THE SPIDER:
EMPEROR OF THE YELLOW DEATH

THE SPIDER

MASTER OF MEN !

®

EMPEROR OF
THE YELLOW DEATH

By Grant Stockbridge

STEEGER BOOKS • 2020

PUBLISHING HISTORY

"Emperor of the Yellow Death" originally appeared in the December, 1935 (Vol. 7, No. 3) issue of *The Spider* magazine. Copyright 2020 by Argosy Communications, Inc. All rights reserved.

CHAPTER 1
WHILE NEW YORK SLEEPS

RICHARD WENTWORTH strolled warily down the night-shrouded reaches of Fifth Avenue. There was nothing of tension in his appearance, top-hat jaunty on his arrogant head, Inverness cape turned back so that it showed the ivory satin of its lining. But his every sense was acutely alert; his superb muscles were as taut as a stalking tiger's.

He was playing a game he loved for its very danger. He was offering himself as fair game for killers he had thwarted once before tonight in a murderous attempt upon a mighty man. It was unlikely that the killers would allow him to go unrewarded... And his reward would be, *death!*

They might spring on him from any darkened doorway, might be lurking just around the next corner. Wentworth hummed a light *aria* in his rich baritone as he paced on, gold-headed cane tap, tapping through the crisp darkness.

Fifth Avenue was as nearly quiet as that great thoroughfare could ever be. The high buildings were black and deserted. No traffic, save now and again the mutter of a night-hawk taxi or the whisper of a limousine gliding home with its burden of wealth and beauty. It was two-thirty o'clock in the morning....

Through Richard Wentworth's happiness in approaching battle there ran a thread of apprehension—not for himself, but for humanity. Years ago, when youth had been hot in his veins,

1

he had killed a man because there had been no other way for
him to prevent a great injustice to one he loved. There had been
no remorse in his soul, only a vaulting joy that a miscreant had
paid the penalty for evil deeds. He had stooped over the man's

Hundreds died like this, wrapped in
a blanket of deathless fire!

body and upon his forehead had traced in blood the figure of
a spider....

On that night, the Spider had been born and since that time,
Richard Wentworth had labored unceasingly—at the sacri-

fice of all normal felicities of love and happiness—to protect mankind against injustice and the depredations of the Under-world. So, tonight, he was a little afraid… afraid that some new peril, some new incredible genius of crime, had arisen to plague humanity anew.…

It was, as yet, only a fear. But tonight, Judge Mahoney's Chinese houseboy had dropped poison into his glass and only Wentworth's super-keen powers of observation had spotted the suspicious behavior and so saved the eminent jurist from death. The Chinese had escaped and Judge Mahoney, shaken with anger, had been unable to ascribe any motive.

So murder had lifted its head, and the head had worn a pigtail and its eyes had slanted upward at the outer corners.…

So it was time for the Spider to fear for humanity. Twice, within his lifetime, there had come deadly menace out of the East. And each time, the streets had run red with blood; each time the Spider had come perilously close to failure that would have meant Chinese dominion over the entire Western world! There was a little silent prayer in his heart now—through all his eager anticipation, that this was some single outbreak—this attempt on Judge Mahoney's life; that it had no universal significance.…

It was in the midst of that half-phrased thought that the attack was made…!

PERHAPS, OCCUPIED with his thoughts, Wentworth had grown a little careless. The warning did not come from his own keen senses, but from behind, where his faithful Hindu body-servant kept watch. Shrill and harsh, Ram Singh's voice rang out, and what he cried made no sense in Wentworth's brain.

"Bhag, sahib!" Ram Singh shouted. "Tiger, master! In the name of the All-High, move quickly!"

Small wonder that the cry seemed mad, utterly incomprehensible. A tiger on Fifth Avenue? But Wentworth's body did not dally in the bewilderment of his mind. As the words impinged on his consciousness—before he fully realized their import—he had flung himself aside. In a single mighty spring, he reached the line of buildings to his left, set his shoulders against the plate-glass window. His two hands gripped his cane as he moved and, even before his back was pressed against the window, the stick had clattered to the pavement and in his right hand there glimmered the dull gray sheen of a cane-sword.

His left hand, dropping the sheath, had crossed his chest and ripped from its holster a forty-five caliber Colt's automatic. And so he came to rest, on guard, while Ram Singh's cry still echoed in the vast silent chasm of Fifth Avenue. He was barely in time. An amazed curse rose in his throat and was stopped by locked teeth.

"Bhag, sahib!" Ram Singh had cried.

And slinking down Fifth Avenue, belly dragging on the cement pavement, great, fierce amber eyes unblinking on its prey, came a Bengal tiger! It was utterly incredible. For a full second, Wentworth wondered if this were not some conjurer's trick out of the Orient, some hoax of hypnotism and the dark night. But he knew it was not. Here in the midst of Manhattan's high stone canyons, he faced a peril more grave than on any *shikar* in Indian wilds. There a hunter sat upon the broad back of an elephant....

"Stand clear, Ram Singh," Wentworth called clearly. There was not the slightest tremor in his voice. He took a long step away from the plate-glass window, then another... and stood, waiting, the tip of his short sword leveled at those malevolent killer's eyes, the automatic braced against his hip. Through his veins, his blood thrummed. In his right temple, where a *dacoit's* knife had left a scar, he could feel a slow, heavy throbbing. He could hear the scrape of the great claws of the beast upon the pavement, hear the deep rumbling of its growl. The black-tipped tail lashed, lashed from side to side. When it became rigid, the tiger would charge....

Wentworth was aware of Ram Singh a few score feet up Fifth Avenue, emerging from the shadows with a knife in his hand. Willingly, the Sikh would plunge into the hopeless battle with that puny weapon, if by that means he could save his master.

"Stand clear!" Wentworth called peremptorily again.

Wentworth suffered no false delusions of his ability to kill the tiger with the automatic, heavy though it was. He might pump all its bullets through the great heart and there would still be strength in the black-striped body to rip him to pieces with fangs and claws. It took a gun with a battering force of five thousand foot-pounds to stop *Bhag*. The automatic struck with six hundred.

Wentworth thought of these things, but only with the back of his brain. Already he had decided upon his course of action. It might bring his death, but it was the only thing possible under the circumstances. When the tiger charged, he would try it. Meantime…. There came to Wentworth, crouching there with his feeble weapons, the sudden certainty that his fears of a new menace to humanity were fully justified. The mere fact that this giant killer had been transported thousands of miles across land and sea for this moment, and secretly transported, was proof that a colossal organization was

behind that abortive attempt upon Judge Mahoney's life. God, O God! Once more the Spider must battle against one of those monsters out of the East; once more he must match wits and strength with the Orient for the very life of the Western world. Once more… if he escaped the tiger's claws!

The tail no longer lashed the beast's sides. It was stiffened behind him, the extreme tip barely moving. The legs were drawn up tautly, ready for the spring. Wentworth's sword arm drew back against his body, poised to thrust. The automatic was heavy against his hip. As if he could read the bestial brain behind those terrifying, unwinking eyes, Wentworth knew the instant when the beast was prepared to spring.

And Wentworth danced forward a yard toward the tiger, and hurled his shouting laughter into the killer's face…!

THE TIGER answered Wentworth's laughter with a roar

and, roaring, it hurled ten feet of steel-muscled death through the air. Wentworth had not attempted to hurt the beast then. He wanted its spring to be straight and true. Nor did he, immediately, leap from its path, for the tiger has the facility of all things feline for twisting in midair, changing its course in mid-leap.

Wentworth's swiftness, earned in years of ceaseless battling for life against enemies who were even swifter than the tiger, did not fail him now. Straight backward he leaped like a fencer recovering from a lunge. The tiger was in the air, great fore-feet reaching out with saber claws for their prey. He could still swerve, but not far, for the strength of his leap was nearing its pinnacle. At that precise instant, Wentworth executed the plan that had sprung full-blown into his brain when he realized the thing he must do….

His right arm jabbed the sword upward toward the tawny breast and, even while that was being done, Wentworth sprang to the left. It was a hairbreadth maneuver. The claws of one out-reaching paw hooked through Wentworth's coat and

RICHARD WENTWORTH

stripped it from his shoulder. It almost jerked him off balance, but he sprang clear.

The tiger's claws, then his head, struck the plate glass window, smashed it into a thousand sword-like fragments as the beast's body went through and into the store. Wentworth's sword quivered in its breast. The heavy automatic in Wentworth's left hand began to speak, not a hurried drumming of wild shots, but even slow discharges that threw accurate lead.

The automatic was emptied and Wentworth's right hand whipped across his chest and pulled a second gun from an underarm holster. He stood, rigidly, with the weapon at ready. In the show window, the tiger thrashed, making the night hideous with its roars. Windows were whipping open in the apartment houses that flanked Fifth Avenue here. A police whistle was going crazy a block away.

For a full thirty seconds, Wentworth stared at the dying beast, then he pivoted toward Ram Singh, who had come to his side. The Sikh bowed, touching both cupped hands to his forehead. There was always worship in his eyes when he gazed on his master, the worship of a strong man for one who has proved himself the greater. Tonight, there was almost idolatry.

"Stay here," Wentworth commanded him swiftly, in Hindustani. "Tell the police I went to a doctor. You do not know which one. This is a circus beast."

Ram Singh was standing, straight and powerful, with his eyes directly on Wentworth's face. "Nay, master, no circus beast. I saw it released from an automobile and…."

A slow smile crinkled Wentworth's eye corners, showed his

even, white teeth. Ram Singh's bearded lips parted. He bowed once more, sweeping cupped hands to his forehead.

"Han, sahib!" he cried, "It is a circus beast!"

With a nod, Wentworth was gone. He had no sword cane now, the shoulder of his dress coat was savagely torn, but he hid it with the cape. His hat was still on his head and his fingers fumbled with a fresh clip for his automatic as he moved at a swift run for the corner of the cross-street just north of him. It was from that corner that the attack had originated. There could be no doubt of that, though his own eyes had detected no lurking forms there when he had gone past. Ram Singh had mentioned an automobile.

He sprang wide of the corner of the building, gun in his fist sweeping the street. It was empty. Slowly he lifted the automatic and thrust it back into its holster. He adjusted the cape about his shoulders, lifted a hand to tap his hat more firmly about his temples. With arm half-raised, he grew rigid, listening.

Somewhere, seemingly within arm's reach, a voice was speaking, a throaty woman's voice that held the slurred and haunting accent of the East:

"Bravery has conquered. Take warning. Even immortality will not save you a second time."

WENTWORTH PIVOTED, hand flashing to his gun again. There was only darkness about him, shadows lay in neat black rows on the pavement where the corner light threw its rays. There was no doorway where a woman might hide; there was no window above him from which she might have spoken. Yet the words lay there in his brain as if inscribed in letters of fire. He had an overwhelming sense of presence, *living presence!* Abruptly, it was gone.

Wentworth straightened, blew out a great breath and only then realized that his head pounded from suffocating lungs, that his forearm ached from the clenching of his fist upon the automatic. He shook his head violently to clear it, then went swiftly along the street to circle the block where the police were congregating with a thin wailing of sirens.

His home was no more than a half dozen blocks away, but, overwhelmed with a sudden, sharp impatience, he hailed a cruising taxi and sped there. The private elevator shot him up fifteen stories and he stepped from it into a foyer of exquisite carpets and lamps which glowed from sheerest alabaster vases.

He cast a swift, searching glance about. A nameless dread stood there with him in the foyer of the duplex penthouse which was his home. So short a while ago he had stood face to face with death…. This foyer was the entrance to a fortress. Walls and door were armored even against rifle fire and those costly lamps concealed loopholes beside which submachine guns always rested on racks. He moved his shoulders as if to discharge a burden, stepped to the door and pressed a hidden bell-button.

Immediately, a port which was covered with bullet-proof glass opened in the door, and the door opened. Jenkyns, who had served Wentworth's father before him, bowed and shut the door with a muffled click of locks. He took Wentworth's cape and hat, made no comment on the torn shoulder of his coat. Wentworth glanced shrewdly at the ruddy old face, impassive beneath the cap of silvery hair.

"What is it, Jenkyns?" he asked quietly.

"A lady to see you, sir," Jenkyns replied.

Wentworth lifted his brows, sighed to the butler to remove torn coat, to fetch him another.

"No name?"

"No name, sir."

Wentworth frowned as he stood, feet braced a little apart, staring at the tapestried portieres which concealed the long drawing-room beyond. There was a strong, self-confident poise to the broad shoulders which evening dress had minimized. His head, the hair crisp and black, cut short to his skull save where it waved back from a part on the left side, was lifted as if in challenge. He was a shade under six feet, but his lithe build, the hard-boned, flat-muscled heft of him made him seem shorter.

Jenkyns returned and settled a tail coat smoothly across his shoulders.

"I shall want Jackson," Wentworth said without expression.

Jenkyns said, "Yes, Master Dick. I'll tell him at once."

WENTWORTH NODDED, moved forward at a leisurely, almost indolent, pace until the length of the drawing room—stretching away to triple French doors which opened on the terrace—lay revealed before him. There was a look of polite curiosity on his strong, tanned face—no more than that. Nor did his expression change when the woman who waited, languorous on his davenport, rose with a rustle of silks at his entrance. A veil covered the lower half of her face, but left her dark, almond eyes exposed to his gaze. Those eyes slanted slightly upward at their outer corners. Her hair was black, but alive with blue lights as she moved gracefully toward him.

Wentworth was conscious of the harder pumping of his heart, of the question that rose in his brain. A Chinese had almost killed Judge Mahoney, a voice obviously Oriental had warned him as he stood there after killing the tiger, and now an Eastern woman waited for him in his apartments.

He felt a curious tautening of his muscles across the shoulders, an invariable warning of danger which he rarely disregarded. It seemed that the body he had driven so often into peril had developed its own means of detecting a hostile presence!

Wentworth bowed from the waist, his eyes never leaving the veiled face of the woman.

"I am Richard Wentworth," he said, his deep, vibrant voice without expression.

The woman's left hand reached out to him, allowing the veil to drop from her face. Somewhere beneath her dark, all-enveloping robe, some bits of silver rang together. Wentworth's ears registered that while he looked into her face with a sharp feeling of discovery.

The woman's nose was thin-bridged and intelligent; her face oval and faintly olive in complexion—but what held him in that first glimpse was the mouth. Long, with mobile lips, deeply dimpled when she smiled as she did now with the languorous, slow allurement of the Orient, that mouth was nevertheless the most cruel that Wentworth had ever beheld! Here was no mere feminine heartlessness. Here was cruelty as stark and primitive as death!

"How can I serve you?" Wentworth asked quietly.

The woman continued to hold out her hand to him and, taking it, Wentworth smiled into her eyes. He let her lead him to the divan but his hand, holding hers, maintained pressure with the first and fourth fingers, the balance of his hand held away—away from the woman's rings. It had seemed to him that her clasp was a bit too convulsive to match with that slow smile. And men had been poisoned with a ring before this!

He freed his hand gently, holding her eyes. Was he mistaken, or had the curtains of blackness there parted for a moment to reveal the feral heart he had read in her smile?

Wentworth proffered the woman a cigarette, lighted one himself when she refused and lounged back upon the cushions. He repeated his proffer of services.

"I do not know," the woman said slowly, speaking for the first time. "I come to serve you."

Wentworth looked at the coal of his cigarette to hide the sudden flame in his eyes. The woman who spoke to him now was the same whose voice he had heard warning him there on the street corner! What was it the voice had said? "Not even immortality will save you a second time."

Wentworth's brain reeled. But what seemed to have happened was impossible. He had come swiftly from the street to his penthouse, yet the woman who had spoken there was here before him. He felt a touch of inexplicable cold and looked up sharply. His heart seemed to hang suspended between beats!

The woman's right hand, concealed until now beneath her robe, was reaching slowly toward him and in it, grasped just behind the jaws, was a tawny adder whose bite meant instant torturous death! The snake's fangs were within an inch of Wentworth's hand...!

CHAPTER 2
THE TURTLE'S CHALLENGE

I F RICHARD WENTWORTH'S face paled slightly beneath the tan, there was at least no jerk of muscles to betray his shock at sight of the deadly snake. In fact, a very slight smile stirred his finely chiseled lips. He looked, not at the viper, but at the woman's face.

"Shall I kill you or the snake?" he asked gently.

The woman's long, cruel lips were smiling, denting her cheeks deeply.

"If you so much as move your little finger," she said, her voice deep, sonorous, "you will die by the bite of the swamp adder."

"It would be a shame," Wentworth said lightly, "to destroy so beautiful, and so interesting, a woman. I think I shall have to kill the snake."

As he spoke, a gun crashed in the room. The woman choked down a scream and gripped her right hand in desperate fingers. Her eyes had whipped wide for an instant, her lips hardening against her small, white teeth. But she controlled herself instantly, did not even look down at the headless snake threshing in death-throes between them on the divan.

"Trickster!" she snarled.

Wentworth got slowly to his feet, bowing to her. Across the room, automatic in his fist, stood a broad-shouldered man in chauffeur's uniform. His face was dead-white and the muscles along his wide jaws knotted and knotted again.

"May I present my comrade-in-arms?" Wentworth said softly, "Ronald Jackson."

The woman stood with her back very straight, long lips smiling.

"Dismiss him," she said, "I have a message for you."

Wentworth shook his head slightly. "I have no confidences apart from Mr. Jackson."

"Afraid!" When the woman sneered, her lips drew back from her teeth.

Wentworth shrugged. "Rather," he admitted casually. "There have been three attempts upon my life within the hour. The Tiger and the Lady."

She laughed, a slow, trilling sound from her throat. Then she shook her head at him slowly.

"You are very astute," she acknowledged. "I thought that your avoidance of the poisoned ring was accidental. You have successfully passed the test. Wang-ba but tried your mettle."

Wentworth smiled politely. *Wang-ba,* eh? Chinese, and Mandarin dialect, too. But it was queer that any man or woman should call himself by that name. In Chinese, it was an epithet of extreme opprobrium. Call a Chinese that and he would slit your gullet in the night, just as a Frenchman will bristle at *fils dune cochone,* "son of a sow," or a German at *Schweinhund,* "swine hound." *Wang-ba* meant "turtle."

"This is pleasant of Wang-ba," Wentworth said quietly, his pronunciation of the difficult *ang* sound equal to hers. "Would you mind telling me a little more of this turtle man, and why he chooses to, as you say, test my mettle?"

He could see that the woman was slightly disconcerted. A faint tint of color touched her cheeks at his pronunciation of the name, which he had spat out epithet-wise. But she kept her smile.

"You mock, Wentworth *san?*"

Wentworth shrugged. "Mummery of this kind always irritates me."

The woman's color heightened. Her lips thinned.

"I think that before the night is over, you will do what is necessary to find Wang-ba and submit yourself."

"Yes?"

"Yes. The method is this. Obtain a row-boat and drift down the East River. You will be challenged. Answer: *The world rests upon the turtle's back!*"

Wentworth listened with his face set in a mold of mockery. "Isn't the turtle afraid the world will crush him?"

THE WOMAN made no answer except her slow smile and moved toward the door, walking with a stateliness and grace which were almost regal. Wentworth turned from her to Jackson and moved his hand in a slight gesture. Jackson's face was still white. His eyes went to the writhing snake upon the divan.

There was indignation and protest against the woman's release in his glance.

From the middle of the room, Wentworth called after the woman. "You'll pardon me if I do not escort you to your car? For some reason, I feel disinclined to brave the night air."

The woman laughed, sending the tinkling sound of her mirth back across her shoulder as Jenkyns opened the outer door. When its closing sent a soft sound through the room, Jackson came sharply forward, stood at sharp attention before Wentworth. These two had been together in the war, Jackson a sergeant, Wentworth a captain, and later, major. Jackson still used the war-time title....

"Begging the major's pardon," Jackson said stiffly, "but are you turning the woman free?"

Wentworth put a hand on Jackson's broad shoulder. "In your care, Jackson," he said. "Jenkyns has thrown the rheostat which will slow the descent of the elevator. You will follow. But, Jackson, do not endanger yourself in any way."

Jackson's face was still rebellious, but he took two steps backward and saluted.

"It will be a long fight, Jackson," Wentworth said as his man strode toward the door. "I'll need your courage—and your marksmanship."

That was all Wentworth's thanks for the shot that had saved his life. But in the bracing of Jackson's shoulders, he read that it was enough. The Spider was well served indeed.... Wentworth hastened to the telephone in the butler's pantry. There was no time now to have the instrument brought to him. He barked a number, stood gripping the phone as if it were his one chance of life. The woman's parting words had been a threat that he could not  ignore. "I think that before the night is over, you will do what is necessary to find Wang-ba and submit...." Yes, undoubtedly a threat. Nor did he need to wonder at its meaning.

Since this Wang-ba had apparently set himself to remove the Spider—or to enlist him as an ally—before really beginning whatever savage business he had in mind, he would overlook no weapon. He would strike at Wentworth through his love! Wentworth heard the automatic ring of the phone begin to buzz rhythmically and he stared fixedly at the instrument as if he would compel the woman he loved to answer—as if he would arouse Nita van Sloan from the depths of her slumber by force of his will.

He stared, and the phone continued to buzz. Despair thrust a cold fist into his breast and squeezed his heart. Nita must answer, she *must!* Not this soon could Wang-ba have learned of his agent's failure on Wentworth himself. Nita's apartment was half across the width of the town, high above Riverside Drive. Good God...!

His thoughts broke off as the phone at the other end of the line rattled. The receiver was lifted. Wentworth breathed out a lusty sigh of relief but it choked off in its midst, strangling him…. For it was not Nita's sweet contralto that answered him, but a sing-song voice intoning in gentle, pious accents *a phrase in Chinese!*

It concluded and the connection was broken gently. Wentworth stood gripping the phone like a weapon, his face twisted with self-mockery and grief. What the Chinese had said was simply: "The world rests upon the turtle's back."

It meant that Nita van Sloan, his beloved, was in the hands of that Chinese monster, Wang-ba…!

WENTWORTH'S PARALYSIS of dread lasted not a split part of a second; then he was frantically signaling the operator. He put through a call for police headquarters, rapidly demanded a radio call to try to trap the Chinese who had answered the phone. It was probable that he had been left there alone solely to convey the message that he had given—but possibly the men of Wang-ba had just seized Nita. It must be that. He would not permit himself to think anything else.

He hung up at once on the police, rang the switchboard of Nita's apartment. There were two men on duty there at all times, a doorman and a hall boy who ran the elevators. If they could slow the Chinese, perhaps the police would get there in time. The phone buzzed on and on into silence and presently the operator broke in to say: "I'm sorry, but they do not answer."

No need to wonder what had happened. The Chinese had made certain of escape by removing the two men beforehand.

Wentworth turned blindly from the telephone, paced with a choppy, impatient stride up and down the length of the drawing-room. He threw open the French doors and stepped out into the crisp coldness of the November night, gazed up at the distant stars. Scarcely a minute did he stand there before he turned again to the house.

It was hard to remain inactive here while, perhaps, Nita was spirited out of her apartment building and away to the stronghold of the Chinese devil who had descended upon the city. But there was nothing else he could do. The wildest driving could not take him to her house in less than twenty minutes. Police would be there in two or three, already were there…. He strangled his impatience, but presently he called the apartment house and this time the gruff voice of a police officer answered. Wentworth's fears were confirmed. There was a Chinese dead in Nita's apartment with a bullet through the body. Nita was gone….

Wentworth went heavily to the drawing-room and through the Gothic arch that led into his music room. He stood there without moving through a long, suffering minute. Then, with wooden hands, he picked up his precious Stradivarius and tucked it beneath his chin. Grief sobbed from the violin…. It was ever thus that Wentworth sought relief from the rack of grief and emotion. How could his brain work clearly when it was mired in pain? He must rid himself of this aching horror that surged within him, and then….

It was more than an hour later that Wentworth replaced the violin in its velvet-lined case. His face was no longer twisted in pain, but firm and hard with the set line of its long jaw, the firm clasp of the lips. He walked to the drawing-room. Ram Singh stood just inside the door. He had discarded his street clothing for the house garb that he particularly

delighted in, white tunic and trousers that came to the ankles of his bare feet, a close turban of the same material. His arms were folded. He did not speak. As Wentworth dropped upon the divan, Jenkyns came smoothly into the room with a waiter upon which stood a bottle of incomparable brandy and a silver pot of steaming coffee. With them, he prepared Wentworth's favorite drink....

WENTWORTH SIPPED from the tall glass absently, his eyes gazing straight before him. Deliberately, he marshaled his thoughts. The attack of the Chinese who called himself Wang-ba had been overwhelming. Only Wentworth's constant habit of caution had prevented his own death and the defenses he had thrown about Nita had not availed. At thought of her, his heart began a high, painful throbbing, but he took tight hold of himself.... Rarely had any criminal begun this powerfully, and secretly. There was no guessing yet what the man's purpose was, nor yet was there any indication as to how he planned to work, unless it be through the murder of prominent men. One thing was certain. Wang-ba was immensely powerful....

Against his bidding, Wentworth's heart and mind turned to the woman he loved. Her sweet face with its proudly lifted chin, the large and intelligent eyes, her smile.... Wentworth cursed raggedly. Before this, enemies had seized Nita to force his obedience, to nullify his fight against them. Always he had ignored the fact that they held hostage the one woman in the world whom he loved, had waged the eternal warfare with increased vigor. It was not that his soul was not torn in two with suffering. But always before him was his pledge of service to humanity, a labor to which Nita also had taken up since the day when Wentworth had confessed his love—and told her why they could never marry. How could the Spider—a man who slew the enemies of the law secretly in the night—take a wife, have a home and children? At any hour, the law might lay him by the heels for anyone of a hundred murders. And the Underworld was his bitter, unceasing enemy....

So, when Nita, before this, had fallen into hostile hands, he had only warned his enemies of the punishment they faced if they harmed her, then had pushed on. Tonight, somehow, he could not steel himself to that courageous stand. He and Nita had battled so long, so perilously. Surely, mankind could not demand this new sacrifice of her, of him? But it was not mankind that made the demand, it was himself—and his pledge.

Wentworth snapped to his feet and the glass, forgotten, crashed to the floor. He could not, would not, longer make Nita suffer thus. He stood glaring straight ahead, fists knotted at his side. The buzzing of the phone did not penetrate his consciousness, but presently Jenkyns, at his elbow, got his attention.

"Master Dick," he said heavily, "the police found Jackson on the street and took him to Bellevue hospital. He does nothing but laugh all the time. They can't get a word out of him."

Wentworth's lips parted drily; his eyes closed.

"It was Commissioner Flynn on the telephone," Jenkyns' expressionless voice ran on. "He wants to know if you'll come to see him in the morning. He said Judge Mahoney was killed in his bed. By an hyena."

Wentworth whirled about, his eyes sharp and piercing. "By an hyena?" he demanded.

Jenkyns bowed apologetically. "That's what the Commissioner said, sir. Said the hyena tore the judge's throat out...."

WENTWORTH STOOD with his hands closing and opening at his sides while anger and hate welled up within him. He had not saved Judge Mahoney, then—only spared him for a more cruel murder. Jackson mad in the hospital, Nita in the hands of the Chinese! Wentworth lifted both clenched fists above his head and a hoarse cry was forced out between his lips. He said no word, but it was his pledge of death to the Turtle who bore the world upon its back.

Jenkyns cleared his throat, his old face distraught. "Commissioner Flynn is waiting, Master Dick. Will you go there tomorrow?"

"Tell him: 'Yes, if I'm alive!'"

He looked over Jenkyns' head as the old butler hurried from the room and his eyes locked with those of Ram Singh, fierce and bitter in his bearded face.

"The man's name is Wang-ba," Wentworth said flatly. "He has kidnaped the *missie sahib.*"

Ram Singh's arms whipped apart and his hand went to the

knife hilt in his sash. His teeth showed white through his beard. "When do we leave, *sahib?*" the Hindu asked harshly.

Wentworth laughed sharply. "At once!"

Wentworth had changed to a suit of rough, dark tweeds and, in the hall, was donning a light top coat when the phone buzzed again. It was Commissioner Flynn and, impatiently, Wentworth took the call.

"Can you come to my office right away?" Flynn asked. "It is of the deepest importance."

"Impossible," Wentworth told him curtly. "The devil who killed Mahoney has kidnaped Miss van Sloan."

Commissioner Flynn made a sympathetic sound. "Why can't we work together? In the last hour, I have had five more reports of murders, all of them as fantastic as possible and all of them of men in prominent political positions: Johnstone, O'Brien, Mullaney. The mayor has been kidnaped…."

Wentworth's eyes were narrowed, gazing blindly at the wall before him. He said quietly, "Anything else?"

"Isn't that enough?" Flynn shouted at him. "Damnation, man, if this keeps up, can't you see that the city will go crazy with terror? Come on down to the office and let's work out some means of fighting the monster behind this."

Wentworth's lips moved in a stiff smile. "I'll see you in the morning," he repeated, "if I'm alive. I have a clue… Keep all of this out of the newspapers if you possibly can. That will eliminate ninety per cent of the terror."

"But, Wentworth…!"

Wentworth whipped away from the phone. "Quickly, Ram

Singh, or Flynn will send his men to stop us. Come, we go to find this Wang-ba."

He strode from the door with the dark-faced Sikh at his shoulder. The visages of both men were bitter with hatred....

CHAPTER 3
THE BLACK RIVER

I T WAS not that Wentworth was callous to the difficulties into which the police had been plunged—the murders and the kidnappings—but his clue was one only he could follow. He would do as this woman had bade him, drift down the East River in a rowboat and await a challenge. Afterwards... well, before this, the Spider had surrendered to his enemies in order to crush them.

As Ram Singh sent the Daimler town car swiftly through the echoing streets, Wentworth sat at ease trying to puzzle out the intentions of the Chinese in these wholesale murders. His mind was at rest concerning Nita for he was speeding to her rescue. The woman had indicated that Wang-ba sought him as an ally. He would not, under those circumstances, kill Nita before a conference had been arranged.

Wentworth shut his mind to those considerations, turned to the murders. Judge Mahoney slain by an hyena; Wentworth attacked by a tiger, by a poisoned ring on a woman's hand, by a deadly snake. Surely, Wang-ba brought with him a multitude of murder weapons! Political assassinations in the city seemed vaguely ridiculous. National murders, the removal of Washington officials, might be understandable, but what did this present outbreak signify?

Abruptly, Wentworth whipped forward in his seat, staring at the street ahead of him. Along the narrow thoroughfare trundled a steam-roller, black smoke rolling from its stack, red light glowing from the fire box. That was curious enough at this hour of the night, but what pulled Wentworth from his reverie was the fact that each of the two men on the steam-roller wore… *a gas mask!*

Wentworth snatched up the speaking tube. "Back, for your life," he snapped at Ram Singh.

The Daimler screeched to a halt, roared into reverse and Wentworth's hand dropped to the cushion on his left, pressed a button hidden beneath its edge. The entire left half of the seat slid forward, revolving as it moved, and revealed in its hollow back a closely hung wardrobe of clothing—the disguises of the Spider. From a drawer, Wentworth snatched two gas masks and tossed one to Ram Singh while he donned the other.

He tapped on the glass, gestured, "Forward, to the steam-roller."

Behind the great goggle eyes of the mask, Wentworth's gaze was hard and merciless. But for his quick, suspicious mind, the Daimler would have rolled past the machine and what would have happened then was abruptly made clear. Along the way that the steam-roller had come, the screams of suffering men and women soared into the cold vault of the heavens. Even as they screamed, some of those bodies sagged forward over the sills only to plunge toward the pavement beneath!

It was clear what was happening. Deadly gas was pouring from the steam-roller! Wentworth's shout of rage was muffled by the mask over his face. His hands flew to the automatics beneath his arms and, the Daimler drawing to a halt beside the lurching steam-roller, he flung to the road. The men upon the machine made no effort to attack him, apparently depending on the gas. WENTWORTH'S LIPS writhed back from his teeth. He was squarely in front of the steam-roller's gigantic main wheel. On its surface, embossed so that it would make impressions in the street as it rolled along, was a neat reproduction of a turtle! If Wentworth had needed any further indication that the gas attack was the work of Wang-ba, this proved it. He waited for no challenge of the men upon the machine. His left gun spat once and the driver pitched forward across his levers. Without a guiding hand, the great roller crunched over the curbing and lumbered toward the brick tenement on its right.

Wentworth sprang to the step, his automatic ready. In his ears dinned the voices of terror-stricken men and women, dying in their sleep of the hellish gas which these minions of the Turtle released through the smoke of their fire. The man tending the fire made no effort to fight off Wentworth. He reached into a box at his side and tossed a half-dozen sticks of some unknown material into the fire, then straightened and stood with folded arms.

Locking his teeth, Wentworth leaped toward the man. This one he would not kill until he had questioned him! There was no resistance at all, but when Wentworth tried to hurry his pris-

He fired three times at the man

who held him prisoner!

31

oner from the platform, he found the man's leg was chained to the bed plate!

A curse rose against Wentworth's locked teeth. He stared at the chain, but knew instantly that he would be unable to break it without long effort. He turned to the box from which the man had snatched sticks to throw into the fire. It was empty except for a packing of sawdust. There were a half-dozen boxes there on the platform, but a swift examination showed that only the one which had held the sticks contained sawdust. Wentworth blinked at his discovery, then the truth about that sawdust-filled box struck him like an explosion.

He sprang to the edge of the platform, motioning wildly to Ram Singh to get the Daimler under way. When he tried to leap to the ground, powerful hands seized upon his leg and held him motionless. He jerked viciously to free himself, but the chained man had wrapped immovable arms about his leg. It was a confirmation of his guess. That sawdust-filled box had been prepared for emergencies. It had contained explosive with which to blast the steam-roller to pieces if it should be captured! And this man had hurled the explosive into the fire box long seconds ago. At any instant...!

There was no time for niceties of warfare. The chained man was already doomed... The automatic in Wentworth's hand jerked three times, and the death grip relaxed. In a single leap, Wentworth was on the running board of the Daimler. Ram Singh did not know what Wentworth had discovered, but he had seen the frenzy of his action and read it correctly. He gave the car all the gas it could take.

Fighting against the violent whip of the wind as the giant car bored into the night, Wentworth managed to get the door open and to drop onto the cushions. As if his weight upon the seat had been the contact, there was a violent, ripping explosion which Wentworth felt as an overwhelming concussion. The car seemed to lift from the road. There was a grinding crash and then long seconds without any noise at all, without any movement....

Impossible to say how long that blankness of mind and spirit continued, but presently Wentworth forced himself up from the cushions on stiff arms and gazed about him. The Daimler was wedged against a tenement house wall. Its engine was dead and Ram Singh was slumped awkwardly across his wheel. The bullet proof glass was not shattered....

WENTWORTH RIPPED off the mask—the explosion would have cleared the air of gas—and bent over Ram Singh. He worked swiftly with skillful hands and within moments, the Hindu quivered back to consciousness. Not until then did Wentworth gaze about him. Up there where the steam-roller had been, a great crater had been torn in the pavement. Two tenement buildings were a collapsed heap of ruins.

Wentworth found that he was clinging to the side of the Daimler for support, that his curses of helpless rage made only dim sounds within his brain. Wang-ba could not content himself with political murders. He was setting himself to wipe out the entire city's population! Wentworth threw back his head in wild laughter. The Spider had dared to think of himself, of Nita. He was punished—punished by the deaths of how many hundreds of persons? On how many streets had the steam-roller clanked its way, imprinting the mocking signature of the turtle in the asphalt?

Still with that sobbing laughter on his lips, Wentworth swung into the driver's seat, pushing the feeble Ram Singh to the other side. The mighty engine started at a touch, the car crunched clear of the tenement and its song of power mounted with speed. There was need of it. Each hour Wang-ba lived would mean more murder, more horror piled on horror in the streets of the city.

Yes, the Spider would keep the river tryst and when he met the Turtle, the Turtle should die!

Slowly, Wentworth calmed as the rush of clean air whipped against his face. Ram Singh straightened in his seat. The East River was very near now, the air turned damp and musty. On a wide, rough street, Wentworth jerked the Daimler to a halt. There was a place near here where a man rented rowboats to fishing parties… It took five minutes to arouse the man, another ten to convince him of the necessity of leaving his house to release the boats.

Wentworth took a rowboat, Ram Singh a larger motor-boat with an outboard engine. It would be noisy, impossible to conceal, but that could not now be helped. Wentworth counted on Ram Singh to do little more than keep an eye on the general direction taken by the boat Wentworth met. Until that time, Ram Singh, too, would row.

Wentworth folded his topcoat and laid it on the stern-sheets of the rowboat, gripped the oars and sent the craft zipping out over the black waters of the river. There was a dauntless strength

in his stroke, a stern anger in his face.... Somewhere out here on the black river, the men of Wang-ba, the murderer, awaited him! WENTWORTH'S MIND whirled with conflicting conjectures as to the reasons behind the atrocities of Wang-ba. Unless the man's purpose was revealed, there could be no anticipation, no preparations, to defeat his moves. Perhaps, if the Spider survived tonight, there would be no need for that....

Wentworth's lips curved in a grim smile. The Spider had small reason to be so sanguine about this meeting. It was true that he had outguessed an agent of the Chinese twice, but on other, more important points, he had entirely failed....

While Wentworth thought, his body, his arms, were moving with the regularity of clockwork, the oars churning the black water. He could feel the surge of the boat at each pull. He threw a swift glance about him. Off to his right stretched the dark shore of Welfare Island on which the City Penitentiary was situated. There stretched the high arch of the Queensborough Bridge whose Manhattan end was at Fifty-ninth street. A tug was panting its way up the river, dragging long, deep-laden barges. But except for that single vessel and Wentworth's rowboat, the river was deserted. The tug's whistle wailed hoarsely, echoed against the steep buildings on each bank. In another hour, the eastern sky would blanch with the dawn….

Wentworth was under the second of the four great bridges that spanned the East River when he became aware of the muted beat of a gasoline motor somewhere near at hand. Instantly, he ceased rowing. Slowly, he twisted about his head to search for the source of the sound. He had no guarantee that Wang-ba did not intend to blow him out of the water at first sight. The whole thing might well be an elaborate trap which was to operate in case all previous efforts failed. It was obvious that Wang-ba had kidnaped Nita even before the Chinese woman had left his penthouse…. Wentworth pulled his oars inboard, drew his automatics and rested his fists upon his knees.

He could see the boat now, a low-lying black craft that creased the water almost without sound. It had lurked in the shadow of the bridge and now it moved quietly toward him, without a light. Wentworth's lips drew thin against his teeth, as a low hail came to him. The voice was that of the woman assassin!

"Who is there?" she asked quietly.

Wentworth's voice was equally undisturbed. His guns swiveled toward the boat. He said in perfectly accented Mandarin dialect: "The world rests upon the turtle's back!" But he used a word for "rests" other than the one the woman had indicated. It implied prodigious, crushing weight…!

The woman's voice harshened. "You will do well not to mock. We are coming alongside."

The black motorboat maneuvered adroitly. Wentworth was conscious of the quickening beat of his heart. If a sub-machine gun were to cut loose on him at this point-blank range.... His fists tightened upon his automatics. The two boats were side by side now and Wentworth could see only two figures, the woman in the stern and a man at the wheel.

The gunwales touched and the woman pinned them together with a boat-hook, deftly handled.

"Come aboard," she said.

"No snakes on the floor?" Wentworth asked mockingly.

The woman did not answer. Wentworth holstered one automatic, picked up his topcoat before he stepped into the motorboat. He was quite sure there was no trickery intended—just yet. Otherwise, there would have been no necessity of his entering the motorboat. He stood in the stern, punching his arms through the sleeves of the topcoat while the woman fended off the rowboat. Instantly, the engine note deepened. Off there in the darkness toward the Brooklyn shore, an outboard motor chugged into life. Wentworth hoped it was Ram Singh....

THE WOMAN crossed to Wentworth's side, her pale face faintly visible in the reflected starlight. He caught the gleam of her teeth and knew that she smiled. "I'm afraid your Hindu will have some trouble keeping up with us," she said, her voice husky, caressing.

Wentworth shrugged, made no other answer. The woman was probably guessing.... The wind was keen over the water and Wentworth sat down on a cushioned side-seat. One automatic reposed in his topcoat pocket.

"Speed is my one desire," he said sharply. "See to it."

Mockingly, the woman lifted her cupped hands to her forehead. *"Han, sahib!"* she said in simulated humility, but there was harshness in the command she snapped at the man forward. Still deeper grew the note of the motor. The prow lifted and the wake turned white. The boat began to skitter along on the step, sometimes seeming to leap entirely clear of the water. Wentworth kept his eyes on the woman.

The sound of the motor, of the boat squattering over the waves, completely drowned out the outboard of Ram Singh's craft. He had no means of calculating the Hindu's speed, but such boats were among the fastest on the water. Success was possible. He settled back more comfortably, turned up his topcoat collar against the edge of the wind. Above the Brooklyn hills, there was the promise of dawn in the sky....

The swift, black boat darted through Buttermilk Channel, bucking a strong flood tide between Governor's Island and Long Island, swept on through the Narrows and clung to the northern shore. The sky was definitely lightening. There was a silver line where heavens and water met. Staring there, Wentworth's wind-burned eyes tightened in surprise. Sloping out of the sea, just breaking the calm, dark surface was a rounded object like… like the back of a turtle!

Incredulously, Wentworth stared, then he laughed sharply to himself, though his surprise and amazement continued. There could be no question as to the identity of the object. It was a submarine! And the motor-boat went directly toward it! A sharp depression of spirits seized upon Wentworth. If his previous speculations on the power of Wang-ba had raised a specter of enormous proportions, they had still fallen far short of the mark. A submarine represented millions of dollars invested. It spoke terrifyingly of the man behind these savage murders. But why, why…?

The dark boat swept on at undiminished speed and Wentworth saw that the submarine was lifting even further above the surface. The woman beside him said nothing, but she was watching him with a smile on her lips. The motor-boat swung a wide circle, headed nose-on for the stern of the submarine. Wentworth saw now what he had not noticed before, an open port in the craft's stern. Into this, with motor cut to idling speed, the boat drifted. There was a slight jar and instantly complete darkness surrounded them. The port had clanged shut behind them. The motorboat was completely inside of the submarine and… there was a downward lurch! The water inside the port sloshed against the sides. The submarine was submerging.

Already, the woman was getting to her feet. A dim yellow bulb flicked on overhead and Wentworth saw that she was stepping to a narrow walkway to the right. The wheelman was busy fastening wide belts over the motor-boat to hold it in place. A small water-tight door opened in the bulkhead beside the walk, and the woman paused beside it. The wheelman finished his task and stepped to her side, went through the door first.

"*Au 'voir*, my friend!" the woman called. She stepped through the door and it closed instantly with a dull, clanging note. Wentworth sprang to his feet. He was locked in a steel, water-tight chamber. His guns were useless now. But why were they imprisoning him here? Merely to wait until Wang-ba was ready to see him? He shook his head. The answer could not be that simple, for....

He stopped his thoughts, listening. The water was sloshing about the boat, but it seemed to him that there was a new note in its sound. With a tightening of his heart, he peered over the side and a muffled shout rose to his lips. Water was pouring into the compartment through a dozen cocks in its sides, swiftly raising the level within the port. Imprisoned in this steel-lined chamber, he was to be drowned, literally, like a rat in a trap...!

CHAPTER 4
THE VOICE OF WANG-BA

SUDDEN AND bitter as was his realization of the death which the Chinese Death Lord planned for him, Wentworth swiftly controlled himself. That one muffled shout was the only sign he gave that he recognized the desperate nature of his situation. He had no means of knowing how deep beneath the surface of the sea the submarine had dived, but he knew it would be futile for him to attempt to plug the score of sea-cocks through which the water poured into his death cell. Even if he had the materials with which to work, the mounting pressure from outside as the submarine sank would render all his efforts futile....

Panic clawed at his heart through long moments while he stood rigid, watching the rapid climb of the water beside the strapped-down boat. One thing he could do and that he did immediately. He unstrapped the broad bands that held the motorboat down. It would rise now with the flood. When it reached the top, he would contrive to capsize it and in the pocket of air formed beneath, he could survive for a while—until mounting pressure robbed him of even that modicum of hope.

Wentworth forced a light laugh from his lips and, removing his topcoat, sat down comfortably upon the cushions of the cockpit. Calmly, he drew out his cigarette case and selected a smoke, lighted up. He took counsel with despair. He was doomed but, he realized abruptly, it was not necessary for him to die alone. He carried always in a compact kit strapped beneath his arms, two vials of liquid which, harmless each in itself, formed the most powerful explosive known when they were thoroughly mixed, trinitrotoluene, the big brother of T.N.T. It had never been used in warfare because of its treacherous nature. Using it in this confined space would mean his own death, but better to use it and destroy this fiend with him than to go alone in slow mental agony.

Flicking the cigarette into the water which now half-filled the chamber beside the rocking boat, Wentworth drew the vials of liquid from the kit beneath his arm. Humming softly, he hunted over the motor-boat until he found an oil can. He emptied and washed it with gasoline from the tank and poured the contents of his two vials into this improvised bomb. He wedged it into the mouth of the gasoline tank, then sat down again in the stern-sheets with his automatic on his knee. A bullet through that bomb would tear open the sides of the submarine as dynamite would a tin can. He lit another cigarette, keeping a keen eye on

LITTLE WHITE FLOWER

the bulkhead door. He thought it likely that he was observed through some secret aperture....

Wentworth's face was completely happy, a smile moving his lips now and again, but his heart was in turmoil. He had no wish to die, though he could face that and calmly if he were sure that he carried Wang-ba to his death also. He could not know that,

of course. The submarine might be merely a link in the chain that led to the Chinese monster. And Nita…. Where was she? Would his death doom her to a life of slavery, of subservience to the will of this creature of murder and doom? He smiled slightly. That was melodramatics! No one could ever subdue Nita save through love. Sooner or later, she would find the means to kill or be killed.

Always, Wentworth had faced this issue of death. Many times he had prepared himself for the end when Destiny turned her face away. Somehow, tonight, he could not achieve the calmness that usually was his. He would not falter when the time came to raise his automatic and put a bullet through that oil can. His gun would lie as quietly in his fingers as if he stood on the pistol range, but his heart, his heart….

WENTWORTH WAS compelled to hunch forward a little now to keep his head from bumping the top of the death cell, and still the water poured in. The air was close. He had, perhaps, twenty minutes before the gunwales ground against the ceiling, ten more after that before the water rushed in and then—why, then, he would shoot!

But why wait? Surely, his case was hopeless. Why not shoot now and have the agony over with? His own pain would be nothing, an instantaneous black-out in a dazzle of white flame. Slowly, as if another hand than his own was in control, he lifted the automatic at rigid arm length before him, his eyes running easily along the barrel. It was superfluous, that sighting. He could have held the automatic on his knee and put seven shots in succession through a target a third the size of that oil can. But he felt a certain pride in the steadiness of his hand. When had it ever failed him in his need? He smiled slowly.

"We'll be together soon, darling," he murmured and his thought was Nita. Whether she was on this submarine and died now, or…. He drew a deep breath, held it, began to squeeze off the shot that would blast him and all the human beings in his craft into the black and red of death....

The voice that spoke was as gentle as a breeze. "What will happen if you shoot that oil can, Wentworth *san?*"

Wentworth was startled, but there was no slightest tremor of a muscle. He merely eased the pressure of his finger upon the trigger, held his gaze along the barrel. He could tell from the slightly metallic quality of the voice that it came through some sort of speaker device, piped into his death cell.

When he answered, his own voice was as incurious, as gentle, as the other. "The whole submarine will split apart," he said. "The can contains about four ounces of trinitrotoluene."

The dim ceiling light blinked out with his last word and Wentworth's reaction was instantaneous. He dropped face down in the cockpit and crawled rapidly, though silently, forward. Within three seconds after darkness fell, he had the oil can in one hand, his automatic in the other. It would not be difficult to form a contact between the two!

"The extinction of the light was accidental," the voice purred. "I am quite sure that by now you have the can in your hand?"

Wentworth smiled in the darkness. Whoever addressed him—and he suspected strongly that at last he heard the voice of Wang-ba himself—was as calm, as deadly, as himself.

"I was assured," the voice went on, "that you had successfully met every test that I had devised. I see now that you have passed this little impromptu arrangement of mine also. We are going to the surface, the chamber will be drained and the inner door opened to you, Wentworth *san.*"

45

It was clever, this instantaneous acceptance of Wentworth's hold upon the speaker. There had been no questioning of his intention and will to destroy the submarine. Wang-ba sought to twist the situation to his advantage.

"By no means," Wentworth replied cheerfully. "Don't let me alter your plans, even by requiring you to return to the surface. I am quite satisfied to remain in this delightfully pleasant place. In fact—" he hesitated, made his voice abruptly harsh, commanding—"I must insist that you keep the light out, that no one enter this chamber or I shall instantly blow up the submarine."

"Shoot then, Wentworth *san,*" said a voice, and its nearness startled Wentworth. This voice came through no microphone. There was a swirling of water beside the boat and an abrupt glow sprang out of the darkness. There, beside the boat, with its chin barely above the gunwale, floated a face, bathed in a greenish glow. "I am Wang-ba," the face said gently, "We are two mighty killers, thou and I. Shall we talk?"

WENTWORTH'S NARROWED eyes studied the face beyond the boat's side, and a cold hatred that exceeded any rage he had ever known mounted to his brain. His automatic centered on the high, broad reach of the forehead and his breath rose, hot and brassy, in his throat.

Intelligence sat upon that head like a crown, but it was a perverted brain. Cruelty was in the thin, smiling lips, feral cruelty like that of the woman. The nose was thin-bridged, almost Occidental, but these things were taken in at a glance, and Wentworth's gaze riveted on the eyes that, even more than the high forehead, dominated the face. They were black and very large. Their stare was as unwinking as that of the tiger Wentworth had killed.

But it was not that which stayed Wentworth's finger upon the trigger of his gun. It was the flaring potency of the will that was behind the eyes. Wentworth had met and battled great men before this, had fought and overcome Chinese who bore in their brains the lore and secret knowledge of the East. But never before, he felt, had he seen such fierce power of mere will. The effect was perhaps heightened by the greenish light which Wentworth guessed came from a flashlight with a tinted bulb fastened somehow just below the chin.

He would kill this man, Wentworth decided. He would kill him before he left this boat, but first there were things to learn. Wentworth did not expect to escape from the submarine alive, but there might be a chance. If he did, he wanted to know the plans of this human beast, lest his confederates seek to carry on after his death.

Wentworth drew in a deep, slow breath. "Enter, Wang-ba!" he said softly.

The Chinese mounted on a rope ladder which, unobserved by Wentworth, had been left dangling from the boat's gunwale. As he stepped over the side, Wang-ba revealed himself clad in garments of rubber which glistened oddly in the reflection of the green light which still sprayed upward over his face. He was tall, several inches taller than Wentworth, and his shoulders were stooped as if from long hours of study. He sat down with a stately bow and the two men looked once more into each other's eyes. The automatic still rested on Wentworth's knee. Wang-ba's weapons, if any, were not in sight.

"There is a young woman," Wang-ba said, his English faultless, scarcely accented, "who is my guest." His eyes were keen on Wentworth's face, but nothing showed there except a polite interest. "I had her brought to me since I was sure you would wish to remain together."

"Kind of you," Wentworth murmured. He intended that Wang-ba should make all the overtures. As matters lay now, Wentworth felt that he held the whip hand. The can of explosive was on the deck beside him where a movement of his wrist could crash lead through it. Wang-ba's face was equally bland.

"If we die here," he went on, "she will die with you. I know that will be a consolation to you."

Wentworth nodded politely once more. So Nita was on the submarine! His gray-blue eyes never left the face of the Chinese, though its cruelty, its satanic power, revolted him.

"These things are trivial," Wentworth said shortly. "You wished to talk to me. Begin!"

WANG-BA BOWED amiably, but there was a flash of his great, overpowering eyes that could not be mistaken. It had been many ages since any man had spoken thus to him—and lived. But he had the patience of the East. He could wait....

"I propose a task that should have been undertaken long ago," he said in his gentle, suave manner. "I am cleansing New York City of wickedness and corruption. The dishonest shall die...."

Wentworth laughed sharply, feeling the violent pound of his heart. "And to that end, you killed hundreds of innocents on the East Side tonight with your infernal gases!"

Wang-ba made a clucking noise with his tongue. "That was distressing, but necessary," he said. "There was a nest of criminals in that region. I am sorry that it was necessary to kill others to find them."

Wentworth leaned forward a little, his hand gripping the automatic on his knees, his knuckles whitening. Their heads were just below the roof and that green glow seemed to exclude the world, to isolate these two here in a little pit of blackness.

"Quickly, Wang-ba," Wentworth said thickly. "My patience grows short."

In the silence that fell between them, his breath, hissing between taut-drawn lips, was plainly audible. Wang-ba wrinkled his face in a little grimace of distaste that seemed strange on his impassive Eastern visage. The shadows of the green light did strange things to his eyes....

"But, surely, Wentworth *san*," the man said, "there is profit in this for you. Even in far China, your name has reached me, your able battles with the Underworld in which you have been equaled, but not exceeded, by this strange being who calls himself the Spider. I was sure that when I came here I would find an able ally in you. Necessarily, I must test you for my own satisfaction, but beyond that…. Will you not join me in my crusade?"

Even beneath the studied suavity of his manner, Wentworth could detect mockery, the deliberate prodding. What the devil, did the man want him to shoot? Wentworth remembered abruptly that the Wang-ba had entered this chamber so quietly that Wentworth had been unaware of his entrance until he had spoken. With a jerk of muscles, Wentworth snatched a fountain-pen flash-light from his pocket and sprayed its diffused beam over the black, lapping waters. The walls of the chamber presented an unbroken surface. He pivoted back to Wang-ba.

"You mock me, Turtle," he said shortly. "If you wish to live, speak swiftly, for my patience grows short, my time even shorter. Let us be done with this mummery. The men you killed were politicians, it is true, but they were of the most honest in the city. Your true plans, at once, Wang-ba. *Don't move.* When I shoot it will be through the brain!"

Wang-ba made a little restless movement with his hands. "You are beyond my comprehension, Wentworth *san*," He reproved. "I come for a quiet talk, come without weapons into your armed presence."

"Until the count of ten," Wentworth interrupted harshly, "I will listen. Then I shoot."

Wang-ba's face twisted into enraged fearful lines. His eyes narrowed, then widened with all their fierce will in their depths. Wentworth felt their force and tightened his grip upon himself, upon his automatic.

"I offer you wealth and the opportunity for service," Wang-ba said, his voice hard, penetrating. "If you refuse, your loved one dies with the ants gnawing at her eyeballs. You yourself shall live only to see her suffering before you emulate it."

Wentworth said softly, "Ah! And tell me now, truthfully, what it is you intend to do."

WANG-BA LAUGHED and the sound was like the grating of a rusty hinge. "I intend to hold New York City for ransom by the nation! Each night that the ransom is delayed I shall behead ten of its officials and wipe out five hundred of its population. The amount of the ransom shall be a hundred million dollars."

Wentworth's tongue was dry with fury. He lifted the automatic so that it was leveled at the high forehead above the satanic face. "A laudable ambition," he said flatly, his voice sounding queer and forced in his own ears. "I regret that you will never fulfill it."

He began to squeeze the trigger and looked into Wang-ba's eyes. There was no fear in their depths, only the explosion of his mighty will. They widened slowly, focusing on those of the man who would kill him. Wentworth felt the impact like a physical force. He smiled slightly, thinking: *I shall not even look away. I shall prove to him that I am the stronger; then I shall kill him....*

The instant the thought echoed like audible words in his

brain, he knew what had happened. This Chinese had put the idea into his brain so that for a few moments longer he would endure the battering of the man's gaze. Wang-ba was supremely confident. Let him but hold this assassin's eyes for a few seconds and not all the powers of hell and earth could make him pull the trigger.

The perspiration sprang out suddenly on Wentworth's forehead. He did not resist Wang-ba's will, but permitted it to invade his innermost being. He breathed deeply, rhythmically and abruptly his voice broke out, full, vibrant. "My will against thine, Oh monster. My will over thine!"

Occult power was not a strange thing to Wentworth. He, too, had lived in the East and there were those who secretly had called him there the Master of Men. He absorbed the will of the Chinese and, absorbing it, turned it back against the man who threw it upon him.

"My will over thine!"

Wentworth's fist was knotted at his side; the muscles writhed and squirmed across his back, swelling his neck as if with fury. His breathing continued deep and rhythmic and his gray-blue eyes blazed back icily into those of the Chinese.

There had been calmness on Wang-ba's satanic face, but that had changed now. His effort of will was apparent in the slow knotting of his brow, in the quickening of his own breath. Wentworth felt a growing triumph though the effort was draining him of power, almost of life itself. Perspiration dropped coldly down his sides. His gun hand came up jerkily, but steadily. He saw Wang-ba's right hand move, the thumb curling over the long-nailed fingers.

"A signal!" Wentworth heard his own words with surprise. "A signal, you cowardly turtle!"

The gun would not come up except in those slow, jerking movements. The hand felt numb, but Wentworth sent all his will coursing along that arm. Wang-ba must die. He must.... The blow against his cheek was no more than a pin-prick, but its effect was instantaneous. The will went out of him in a stream, as through a gashed artery. The gun dropped thuddingly from his hand and he felt himself falling, falling toward the bottom of the boat. It seemed to take hours, that fall....

Before Wentworth reached the floorboards, he saw Wang-ba stoop and retrieve his automatic. The explosion was the clap of doom and darkness swooped upon Wentworth's brain. He did not even remember hitting the bottom of the boat. So this was death....

CHAPTER 5
IN THE MONSTER'S TOILS

NITA VAN SLOAN'S prison on the submarine was a tiny cubicle just the length of her bunk. She could take two and a half short paces down its length and back again. She took them, over and over. She stopped before the mirror that was fastened to the wall above a tiny lavatory and stared at her face.

She was terribly white, her violet eyes seemed twice their normal size and her bronze-lighted curls were awry. Absently, her hands went to her hair. Her shoulders slumped a little. God, it was so hopeless. She had not even known that Wentworth had started on some new case, otherwise she would have been on her guard. She would not have even slept. As it was, she had had time for only one shot into the press of Chinese who had swept down upon her, then there had come a sickening, sweet odor and darkness.

Aboard the submarine, a tall, gaunt Chinese with a hatefully cruel face had smiled upon her.

"Your lover will be with you soon," he had told her, then had her thrust into this cubicle. That had been three, no four, hours ago by the tiny watch upon her wrist. For a little while, she had prayed that Dick Wentworth, her Dick, would come, but instantly she had repudiated that cowardly wish. If Dick came, he would come as a prisoner. She did not want that. He must remain free to battle this monster out of the East.

Her thoughts had advanced no further than that when the door was thrown wide and a Chinese bowed with an impassive face and indicated she was to go down the corridor. She went with her head high, her eyes proud.

It was insufferably hot in the submarine. Tiny fans whirred everywhere and Nita knew, because the motors no longer were noisy, that the craft was proceeding on its electric motors, which meant it was submerged. How could Dick find her here?

She entered the forward control room and a little cry spurted up in her throat. She did not even see the gaunt, stoop-shouldered figure of Wang-ba. She saw only the lifeless body of Dick Wentworth thrown carelessly on the floor. She flung herself down, took his head in her arms. There was a tiny feathered dart sticking out of his left cheek. With a gasp, she tore it loose and a bead of blood oozed out of the wound and rolled down his cheek. Thank God! He still lived!

"I told you," came Wang-ba's gently mocking voice, "that he would be with you soon. I regret that his impetuosity made it impossible for him to arrive in better condition."

His voice crackled then in Chinese and two men caught up Dick's body. Nita scrambled to her feet, white hands clenched at her sides. She fought down a desire to scream, to fight for possession of Dick's body, but she knew how that would please Wang-ba, and she mastered herself. It was by a strenuous exertion of will that she held her head high. She was helpless now, utterly helpless, but her time would come. God, it *must* come! And when it did, this monster would pay!

She followed the men with Wentworth's limp body. They placed him on her bunk, and it was with a prayer of thanks on her lips that she heard the door close behind them. Feverishly, she went to work to revive Dick. His heart beat, sluggishly, without vehemence. She never knew how long she had worked before his eyelids quivered and lifted. Nita flung herself upon his chest and the sobs she had choked back so long rose up without restraint.

Dick's hand touched her shoulder and hovered there. Finally she lifted her head, gazed into his face. When she did, a harsh breath escaped her. This was Dick, and yet the face was not that of the man she loved! There was no firmness in the line of the jaw and the lips seemed flabby and without will. Even the eyes were dull and hopeless.

"Dick," she whispered, "Dick, for God's sake, boy, what is the matter?"

WENTWORTH PUSHED himself up from the bunk and looked with lackluster eyes about the room. "The matter?" he said heavily. "The matter is that we are beaten. We are helpless. We are in the power of a greater man."

Nita shrank back, staring at his slouching shoulders, his hanging head. There was a parrot-like quality about his words, as if he were repeating a well-learned lesson. A little moan rose up from her heart. She knew, without analysis, what had happened. By drug—or hypnosis—this Chinese beast had robbed this brave man of hers of his will, of his courage! Dick Wentworth never gave up hope while there was life in his body, but now, now…. Nita's head sagged. Tears stung her eyes.

As if her grief were an echo of his own thoughts, Wentworth made no effort to comfort Nita. He continued to sit with sagging shoulders upon the bunk until her sobs stopped of themselves. That was soon. Nita could not permit herself despair. She began to plead with Dick, seeking to set her own attraction above that of the man who had put his will upon Wentworth.

Dick seemed to recognize vaguely what had happened, but his own efforts were futile. Perspiration beaded his forehead as he fought to concentrate his own limitless powers of recuperation and will. A merely mental control could never have been established over him. This semi-coma was a result of hypnosis imposed on him while the drug carried on the dart was coursing in his blood. Yes, Wentworth tried to struggle, but he was like a man whose vital power has been drained. The will was there without the strength. Finally he slept, and Nita, gazing down at him with sorrowful eyes, had to bite back the whimpering despair that had her by the throat.

Many times, while Dick lay helpless beneath enemy bullets or captive to the enemy, she had taken over the reins for the Spider and ably guided his men. But never had the battle seemed so sure to fail. She sank down beside the bunk, rested her weary forehead against Wentworth's dangling hand.

Abruptly, the hand hardened into a fist and Wentworth came to his feet. He stood in the middle of the tiny cabin, staring unseeingly ahead of him.

"Come," he said harshly, "The Master calls!" He went to the door, and, with a pitiful smile on her lips, Nita followed. Dick had called another man "Master!" He who was himself the master of men! The door opened beneath Wentworth's hand and he turned unhesitantly down the corridor to the control room where first Nita had faced Wang-ba....

The many instruments upon the steel walls were hidden behind silken drapes of a bilious yellow-green and Wang-ba himself was seated upon a throne shaped like a giant turtle. The only light in the chamber came from the greenish glow that suffused his face. Nita knew all this was mummery, but a shudder jerked at her shoulders. Though he had used cheap, theatrical effects, this man had overcome the Spider!

Wentworth, she saw, was bowing submissively before the throne. Deep, throat laughter bubbled from Wang-ba's lips, but

Wentworth lifted a clenched hand.

"I will kill the Governor!" he vowed.

his-greenish face remained impassive. He looked at Nita, but he spoke to Wentworth.

"My faithful one," he said gently, "I have called you to perform a slight task for me."

Wentworth bowed once more, attentive, eager.

"Governor Kirkpatrick is my enemy. Therefore he is your enemy, is he not?"

"He is my enemy," Wentworth intoned, and a grating harshness touched his voice.

NITA STARTED at the hatred that sprang full-born into Wentworth's face. Her hands twisted, writhed before her. This was impossible; this was a thing that could not occur. Kirkpatrick and Wentworth were intimate friends of long standing. They had battled side by side through many a perilous night, had defied death a hundred times over for each other. Yet now, at a word from this monster, Wentworth hated—actually hated bitterly—his friend. There could be no doubt of it. Bitter detestation was there in every line of Wentworth's face, in every inflection of voice. Nita swayed a little, lifting her clenched hands to her throat.

"Yes," Wang-ba purred gently, "Kirkpatrick is your enemy; therefore you will kill him. You will kill the governor for me, will you not, my faithful one?"

Wentworth lifted a clenched hand above his head. "I will kill the governor!" he vowed. It was a chant of joy as it issued from his lips.

Nita sprang before him, caught that fierce, clenched hand and dragged it down. "Dick, for God's sake!" she whispered. "Have you gone mad? Kirkpatrick is your dearest friend. This man has hypnotized you. You *won't* kill Kirkpatrick!"

There was a shrinking within her at the gloating hatred which distorted Wentworth's face, but she forced herself to speak on, to entreat with him.

"Kirkpatrick is your friend," she repeated firmly.

Wentworth laughed, gratingly. "Kirkpatrick is my enemy. I shall kill him, "

Nita whirled from this man she no longer even knew, reached out pleading hands to Wang-ba.

"In heaven's name," she begged, "don't make him do this thing. He and Kirkpatrick are most intimate friends. You'll ruin his life…" She paused, recognizing in the pathetic weakness of her words, the utter futility of the petition she made. What did this yellow monster care for a wrecked life? It would appeal to his twisted Eastern sense of humor to send a man to kill his best friend.

Wang-ba answered, smiling gently: "If I ordered him to kill you, my dear, he would do it without question!"

"Do it!" Nita hurled at him. "Go on and do it! I tell you this: If he kills me, he will afterward kill you. My dead eyes will undo the spell you have laid upon him. You know that. You will not dare to order him to kill me."

For a long moment, Nita hoped desperately that she might enrage Wang-ba enough to make the monster order Dick to attack her. Anything—anything!—was better than this. If Dick were to go on being the slave of this monster, she did not wish to live. And there was a chance that what she predicted would come to pass. There was a strong psychic bond between Dick and her, so very close had they become through their many travails. It was more than mere love. It was a union of souls…. Suddenly, Nita was very tired. And she knew she wished no such thing as she had rashly demanded. That was a coward's way and whatever charge might be laid against her soul, it was not that she was craven….

She became aware that Wang-ba was leaning forward slightly with the black flame of his eyes upon her. "You are a brave woman," he murmured softly. "I wonder if you are brave enough to do a little thing I ask. If you will, this man shall not be required to kill his friend."

A thrill of hope shot through Nita, but she cautioned herself against letting it show. Wang-ba could be trusted no more than a temporarily quiet snake. If she won surcease for Dick, it would be only for a while, but it might be that the spell upon him would wear off… She lifted her head and looked contemptuously upon the green face of the Chinese.

"You intend treachery," she said clearly, her mouth scornful, "but I will hear you."

Wang-ba laughed softly, once more without movement of his face. He delayed words for a long minute, looking her over with a slow calculation that brought the blood hotly to Nita's face.

"Speak, beast," she said with a furious tremble in her voice. "And speak quickly!"

But Wang-ba would not be hurried. She saw a spasm of rage touch his ebon eyes and depths in them seemed to open— depths of feral cruelty. Nita gasped.

"Beware, little white one," Wang-ba said softly. "Beware lest you anger me beyond my patience and I forget how well you can serve me."

Nita lifted one shoulder in a little shrug of indifference she did not feel and turned toward Dick. He stood rigid and unmoving, his face an expressionless mask. The sight of him weakened her. She did not relax her hauteur, but she turned back to Wang-ba and stood waiting. He nodded as if what he saw pleased him.

"I would rather," he began slowly, "have Governor Kirkpatrick alive than dead. If you will promise to deliver him into my hands, Wentworth *san* shall not be required to kill him."

As Wang-ba finished, he clapped his palms softly together. Two men seized Nita's shoulders.

"You shall have half an hour to make your decision," he declared. The audience was over. Nita was whipped backward and away....

NITA WAS half-stunned as she was thrust into her cabin, too dazed even to hurl defiance and hatred at Wang-ba. How could he propose such treachery? She dropped down on her knees beside the bunk where Wentworth had lain and clasped her hands beneath her bowed face. She did not consciously pray, but she did commune with herself. Slowly, the burning anger left her and clarity returned to her brain.

When finally she rose to her feet, the half-hour was nearly past and she had just begun to think. At the mere idea of what Wang-ba proposed, anger gnawed at her brain, but she controlled it resolutely. She knew that Wentworth would not have considered the proposition for a moment, knowing the treachery of the East, and more than that, being unwilling to let personal considerations drive him to so base a deed. Nita recognized that fact humbly, but she was a woman. She loved....

Nita was completely at peace with herself when the door opened and a coolie with a scar-twisted eye gestured for her to go once more into the presence of Wang-ba. Her decision was not completely made, but she had little doubt that when she looked again on Dick's soulless face, she would do Wang-ba's will....

When she entered the room, it was empty save for Wang-ba. Her eyes flew frantically about.

"Where is Dick?" she demanded sharply.

Wang-ba looked at her without words and Nita took two quick steps forward, her arms bending, fists clenched.

"Where is he?"

"He is safe, if you obey," Wang-ba said softly. "He has a half-hour start of you on the way to call on Governor Kirkpatrick. If he arrives there first, Kirkpatrick dies. If you get there first...."

Violent words rushed to Nita's lips but she held them back. Her clenched hands dropped to her sides. "You make the odds... difficult," she said dully. "I do not even know where Kirkpatrick is."

Wang-ba's eyes widened with pleasure. He drew a small fan of silk and ivory from his wide sleeve and began to flutter it gently beneath his chin.

"Not at all," he said gently. "Not at all. I have sent Wentworth *san* and twenty of my men to the Pelham home of the Governor.

They will wait there until you bring the Governor there. If there is any treachery, Wentworth strikes… and recovers to realize what he has done. If Kirkpatrick submits, you may all return here peaceably together."

Nita moved a hand impatiently. "You are wasting time," she said, her voice suddenly hoarse. "Suppose the Governor goes there without me…."

Nita had not dared to hope that she could save Dick, but now there seemed a chance, in spite of what Wang-ba said. The Chinese lifted a hand languidly, its long nails with their guards of jade and gold glinting in the greenish glow. To men behind Nita, he spat swift words in Chinese, few of which Nita could catch.

"A word of warning before you go," Wang-ba said to Nita. "At the first sign of treachery, of an effort to surround the house or to rescue your lover… Wentworth dies. You understand? Though he can be of much service to me, I will sacrifice him at the first sign of such treachery." The black eyes held Nita's through slow, thudding heartbeats of time. He nodded abruptly. "You may go."

NITA WAS surprised to find daylight when she was taken from the motorboat port of the submarine. The crisp autumn air fanned color to her pale cheeks, but not even the wine of sea-wind could restore the sparkle to her eyes. She had only her wits to combat the fiendish intelligence and multiple preparations of Wang-ba. Her own meager strength against twenty, a hundred men and God alone knew what instruments of death and torture. But she must win, she *must…!* It was not only that

Dick's life was forfeit. She realized abruptly that the power this man represented overshadowed the very sun of the Western world. To kidnap or kill Kirkpatrick was his present plan. The Mayor of New York was already his prisoner, he had said. Wholesale murder....

Nita threw off the doleful thoughts with a bracing of her proud shoulders. She looked about and realized that she was speeding up the East River. Hell Gate lay ahead; then Pelham and her interview with the Governor. What was she to do when she came face to face with the man who had been Dick's friend and hers through so many perilous hours? Nita shook her head miserably. She couldn't, even with Dick's life at stake, lead the Governor into such treachery! But she must....

She looked up as the boat jarred faintly and saw that it lay against a dock. She glanced about and recognized City Island. The automobile that waited was familiar and she realized with a start of pain that it was Dick's own Daimler. Vague hope began to stir within her. There were secret compartments in its tonneau which might not have been discovered. There were weapons, a score of the Spider's mechanical and chemical devices. She was careful to hide her elation as she was led forward....

At the door, a hand at her elbow stopped her and she turned to find herself looking into the face of the Chinese woman. The long, cruel lips smiled slowly.

"Remember, at the first treachery... your lover dies!"

The woman sauntered away and Nita stumbled blindly into the car, which instantly began its smooth forward glide. She sat forlornly while miles whirled past. Alone, against Wang-ba!

Even now she was under surveillance. The man at the wheel was a Chinese. As if he felt her eyes upon him, his head turned slowly and he lifted a long-bladed knife into view. Within her head rang, with an effect of spoken words, the woman's message: "Remember, at the first treachery… your lover dies!"

Nita looked about sharply, lifted the speaking tube. "Where are we going?"

"To Pelham," the man's words were harshly accented, almost unintelligible, "So you can see master tell true."

SHE DROPPED the speaking-tube. She was to see Dick again, for a few seconds; then she would be called on to betray the Governor with a knife against Dick's throat to insure her faithfulness to Wang-ba… But this was the counsel of despair. She must remember that, though Dick would die if she were treacherous to the Chinese; Dick and she and Kirkpatrick would die ultimately if she obeyed. There could be no question of Wang-ba's intentions. But how, in the name of heaven, could one lone woman defeat him?

The car turned into the drive of the Governor's Pelham mansion and, as she mounted the steps, the door opened. A Chinese led her through the broad hall that she remembered so well to the Governor's office. A cheerful fire of channel coal popped and breathed flames in the hearth. Nita stood in the middle of the room. A portiere was pulled aside behind the desk and Dick stood there, rigid as a statue, with an automatic in his right hand. There was a Chinese beside him with a knife. As clearly as if Wang-ba spoke, Nita got the message. At the first sign of treachery here, two men would die, Wentworth and Kirkpatrick.

A hand touched Nita's elbow and the Chinese led her back to the Daimler. He bowed, holding the door. "The Governor is in New York," he said, without expression. "He holds many conferences today. You have until nine o'clock tonight to get him back to this place."

Nita sank back into the cushions, the door snicked shut and the Daimler's fat tires popped over the gravel drive, hit the smooth soundlessness of the asphalt and turned cityward. Nita closed her eyes, no longer even thinking. She would bring the Governor to Pelham, she *must!* But before then, something surely would happen to point the way for her. Dear God, how was it possible that every hope should fail?

The Daimler drew to a halt and a *chasseur* opened the door. Nita alighted and found herself in the tunnel entrance of the Waldorf-Astoria hotel, where the Governor was holding his conferences. She braced herself. She had a part to play, the life of the man she loved depended on her histrionic ability… She sent her name up to the Governor and, ten minutes later, his secretary appeared to escort her into his presence.

Nita went into the office of the friend she must betray. There was a gay smile on her lips….

CHAPTER 6
NITA'S SACRIFICE

GOVERNOR KIRKPATRICK came gravely to his feet as Nita advanced into his office. He smiled, his blue eyes warm, as he held out both lean hands to her.

"We've been worried, Nita," he said, his clipped metallic delivery even sharper than usual, certain evidence of his concern. "Dick promised to see Flynn this morning and I had planned to be there, too. He didn't show up. Ram Singh has entirely disappeared and Jenkyns knows nothing—beyond the fact that Jackson was in Bellevue. You can imagine...."

Nita laughed. "Yes, I can imagine, Stanley." Her eyes inspected his long, saturnine face, the determined compression of the lips beneath the spiked ends of his militant mustache. There were touches of gray above his temples. A dignified, grave man, who rarely smiled save in friendship... and often smiled on Dick Wentworth. How could she betray this strong one into the hands of that damnable Chinese?

"Where is Dick?" he demanded eagerly. "Outside? It would be like the scoundrel."

Nita's smile stiffened on her lips. Her eyes were artificially bright, her words unconcerned. "Oh, he's around. I have a message for you, but... it's private."

Kirkpatrick's heavy, smooth brows drew together on a vertical crease. He nodded, brisk business all at once. His secretary was inconspicuous in a corner. The two state troopers who were rarely out of the sound of his voice, kept guard on each side of the door. Kirkpatrick nodded sharply to them.

"Cushman, leave me, please," he said to his secretary.

As the door closed softly behind them, he turned to Nita, his mouth a harsh line.

"Well, Nita?" he asked.

Easy now for Nita to say that Dick was at his Pelham place and that he wanted Kirkpatrick to come there without delay, that for certain reasons he had not explained to her, he could not come into the open himself. Kirkpatrick would go without question. Easy, yes, to lead this fine man to his death. Nita opened her lips… and closed them again. Her eyes fell before the relentless demand of Kirkpatrick's, and she walked past him to the wide window that gave on Park Avenue, a half-dozen stories below.

Kirkpatrick did not follow, but she knew that his eyes were upon her back. She could see him as if she looked on him, standing straight and commanding, with his erect back and his high-flung head. But another figure superimposed itself on her mental vision, an erect man, too, with a fine, manly face, his blue-gray eyes so often twinkling, the half-mocking quirk of his brows.

NITA VAN SLOAN

Her head dropped and a muffled sob hit against her lips. Oh, God, *Dick!*

Kirkpatrick's hand touched her shoulders gently. "What is it, Nita?" he asked, the sharpness, the brittle command gone.

She twisted about and put her hands on Kirkpatrick's chest, looking up into his glittering blue eyes. Her teeth set on her lips. It would be so easy… She shook her head, making the bronze curls quiver beneath the brim of her close little fur toque.

"Dick… Dick is a prisoner of the Chinese man who," her words faltered, "who calls himself Wang-ba."

"Where?"

NITA COULD feel Kirkpatrick's chest muscles stiffening beneath her hands. She realized abruptly that she could not betray Kirkpatrick into the hands of that beast. Dick would rather die a thousand deaths than have it happen. An agony of apprehension shook her. Suppose… suppose Wang-ba had this place watched—had methods of hearing what went on in the office of the governor? She smothered a cry of fear. She turned her eyes to Kirkpatrick's in a desperate appeal.

"Come with me to your Pelham place, Stanley?" she asked.

Kirkpatrick was still frowning, trying to read the thing that was in her eyes. "I don't understand," he said gruffly. "Why?"

"Please, Stanley," she said, her words a swift rush. "Please, come, and don't ask reasons. It is… terribly important."

Kirkpatrick stared at her, then turned away abruptly and took a turn up and down the office, came back to her. "There's something here I don't quite understand," he replied, clipped voice decisive again, "but I'll go. I have a feeling that it is every bit as important as you say."

"Oh, it is, Stanley, it is!"

Kirkpatrick nodded his long head, with its high-clipped, black hair that gave him so brisk an appearance, strode to the desk and began pushing buttons, snapping orders. Five minutes later, beside Kirkpatrick in his Lincoln town-car, Nita was speeding toward the Pelham Manor mansion. She sat twisting her white hands. She need only keep quiet now and she would have fulfilled her part of the bargain, Kirkpatrick would be in the power of the Chinese and his twenty men; Dick would be safe… But only temporarily! Only until Wang-ba decided upon a new errand for the two of them. Staring straight ahead of her, she began to talk.

"I was afraid there might be a leak somewhere in your office," she said woodenly. "I couldn't tell you there."

She told him everything then. Kirkpatrick heard her without comment and even when she had finished, he held his peace. Nita looked at his face anxiously, but she could not read it. The saturnine lines had drawn longer, and the mouth was harsh as a steel blade. They rode in silence while the Lincoln wove through traffic behind the purring sirens of the State troopers, up through the Bronx and toward the shore of Long Island Sound.

Kirkpatrick pushed out a slow, noisy breath. "It's a problem, isn't it? I've been trying to think what Dick would do under the circumstances and I can't. I don't see how I can surrender myself to Wang-ba, although that is my inclination."

Nita's hand grasped his arm. "Oh, Stanley, of course you can't!"

He turned a twisted smile toward her. These two had had their bitter moments together before this. There had been the day when Nita had gone to Kirkpatrick to petition a pardon for Dick, awaiting execution on a framed charge of murder. She had pleaded, then she had threatened with a leveled gun…. And Kirkpatrick had held true to his oath and his personal conception of unswerving duty.

"You think I wouldn't?" Kirkpatrick asked, his voice suddenly hoarse. "If it wasn't that it would give that beast so great a hold on the state… I might resign and then surrender." He laughed sharply. "He would know the trickery at once, of course, this Chinese friend of ours, and we would all suffer."

HE SANK back against the cushions, his face drained and tired. "I wish that once, when Dick needed me, I could answer as I would like without a thought except that he needed me. It seems I never will, doesn't it, Nita?"

He went on, then, to tell her what had happened during the hours since Dick had disappeared. Five hundred people had been killed by a strange gas and on the streets had been found that strange image of a turtle, crushed into the pavement. The explosion….

"Dick stopped them," Nita explained dully, "and they blew themselves up. A steam-roller, gas in the firebox."

Kirkpatrick's laughter was painful and it choked off. "We need Dick so. We need him," he whispered. "Perhaps, that would be justification for me."

Nita objected, "No!"

The Governor's shoulders sagged. "At noon, we got a demand from this Wang-ba. He declares that the city is in a state of siege, that anyone attempting to leave will be killed. He kept his promise. Trains attempting to run on schedule burst suddenly into flames and practically everyone aboard them died. The *Rex*—that big Italian liner, you know—blew up in the Narrows. So the harbor is blocked. The railroad tunnels under the river are blocked by trains that burned there. We closed the Holland Tunnel and the George Washington Bridge. No use giving the devil more opportunities for slaughter."

Nita heard these things with mounting horror. Her soul was besotted with terror for Dick and she saw all things in relation to that. If the Chinese was powerful enough to hold the city in the palm of his hand, what chance did Dick have to escape?

"… a hundred million ransom," Kirkpatrick was saying. "And each night that we delay, he will kill a section of the populace. The five hundred last night, he says, was a warning. Tonight, it will be a thousand, tomorrow night two thousand. Also the heads of ten public officials will be sent to military headquarters." Kirkpatrick turned to Nita. "I put the city under martial law, of course. This morning, the heads were those of members of the Municipal Assembly." A wry smile twisted his lips, "I've thought for a long time that their abolition would be good for the city, but I never meant anything like this."

The Lincoln was rolling through Pelham Manor now, the Governor's house was not far away. Nita turned to him. "What are we going to do, Stanley?" she asked.

Kirkpatrick reached forward and opened a panel in the back

of the front seat, drew out two heavy automatics and a few extra clips of bullets. "I took a tip from Dick's car," he said dryly. He handed one gun to Nita and she checked it mechanically, found there was a bullet in the chamber and that the weapon was cocked, then thumbed on the safety and let it drop in her lap, Kirkpatrick watched her efficiency with curious eyes, then let his own gun rest on his knee.

"I haven't any plan," he said dully. "I'll go into my office, of course. They can't object to my usual precautions—my secretary and the troopers outside the door. If you'll pull down the drapery behind which you saw Dick and the Chinese with the knife, I'll guarantee to kill the Chinese before he can stab Dick. After that, I don't know."

Nita nodded slowly. "I suppose there's nothing else we can do. Dick is hypnotized, remember. Under drugs of some kind, too." Her face had, usually, an austere beauty—a warm loveliness when it softened with a smile—but now it was very pale. Her mouth was tight and rigid and her eyes were dark pools in which fires slumbered. "I'll take care of the Chinese," she announced, matter-of-factly.

Kirkpatrick laughed suddenly. "By God, Nita, we'll take them," he said. "I don't wonder any more at Dick's exploits. He has you to support him!"

Nita said nothing and gravel popped under the tires, the Lincoln drew to a halt before the door of the Governor's Mansion. The chauffeur jumped out and threw open the door. Kirkpatrick alighted and handed Nita down. They looked at each other and Nita's lips smiled slowly. They went into the house together....

INSIDE THE big, dim hall of the mansion, Nita began to chatter gaily. She was surprised at her ability to dissemble. If there was a slight shrillness to her deep contralto, the Chinese would attribute that to the part she played for them.

Kirkpatrick responded gravely as was his wont, handing stick and hat with his topcoat to the white-faced butler whom the Chinese obviously had terrified, and opening the door of his office for Nita, bowed her in.

Irresistibly, Nita's eyes went to the curtain behind the desk where Dick had stood when last she entered this room. Was he still there with that Chinese holding the bare steel of his knife ready? She would have to find out before she betrayed her intentions by tearing the arras down. She felt a tightness in her chest against which her heart pounded like a captive thing. Her breath came irregularly. Kirkpatrick was talking:

"... kind of you to persuade me to come here, Nita. I am sure I will be much safer here than at the hotel, especially since it's the last place on earth I'd be expected to come. Cushman, pull aside some of those curtains, will you, please. It's rather dark...."

Cushman began spreading the curtains. Nita, having walked to the desk with Kirkpatrick, moved toward a window.

"It is dark," she agreed. "The sky must be clouding up. I didn't notice when we came in... "Her hand was on the curtain behind which Dick and the Chinese had been hidden. It came to her suddenly, overwhelmingly, that they would no longer be there. Wang-ba would expect some slight treachery. It would be inevitable in one who, like Nita, served so unwillingly… There was a crashing discharge of guns in the ante-chamber. Cushman uttered a strangled curse and Nita whirled about. The secretary was dashing toward the outer door, with a revolver in his hand.

"Stand back, Cushman," Kirkpatrick ordered. There was a quality in his voice which invoked instantaneous obedience. Nita was clinging to the drapes, hoping against hope that the troopers outside there had triumphed. They all waited like that, Nita and Kirkpatrick and Cushman with guns in their hands and eyes on that thick, dark portal that connected with the next room. It opened slowly and through the crack, a bony, yellow hand reached in. It was empty except for an envelope. The hand waved the envelope….

"Get it, Cushman."

The secretary went forward behind his gun, took the message and the Chinese hand threw the light switch beside the door and withdrew. Bracket lights around the walls flicked on, burned brilliantly an instant, then the bulbs popped, one after another with a thin, explosive tinkling.

"Smash the windows!" Nita heard a voice cry and realized it was her own. "Smash the windows! It must be gas!"

As she spoke, she felt… *felt the curtain stir!* With a glad cry, Nita whirled, tearing at the portiere.

"Smash the windows!" she shouted again and heard a chair crash through glass. The portiere came down and she saw a knife flash upward. The gun in her hand spoke like thought. Dick had taught her to shoot like that and she had practiced until her accuracy was almost as unerring as his own, until the automatic became merely an extended nerve-end of her being. Her bullet sped not at the man behind the knife, but at the knife itself. She knew that no lead, however well placed, could check that thrust, unless it delivered its six hundred foot-pound shock toward turning the blade.

SHE COULD not even see clearly when she fired, just the flicker of the knife. Then the curtain completed its fall and she saw a Chinese doubled over a smashed hand, trying to claw a weapon from his sleeve. Deliberately, she fired again and staggered back as she saw the back of the man's skull carried away by her lead. She felt nausea strike like a hammer and the sound of more glass smashing came to her faintly. She fought to focus her eyes on the other figure behind the curtain, on Dick. He held a gun in his right hand and he had not moved throughout the turmoil about him. But now, Nita saw, he was beginning to act. He was lifting the automatic with a slow and awful steadiness. Nita's eyes riveted on that lifting weapon.

"Dick, old man!" That was Kirkpatrick's hearty voice. "Thank God, you're all right. *Dick!*" Horror was in that last word and Nita knew, without being able to see where Kirkpatrick was, what was happening. That lifting automatic was pointing directly at the Governor! At Wentworth's dearest friend!

Nita's sickness gripped her with weakening fingers, but she fought toward Dick. If he shot his friend… Her own gun was a useless thing. It fell from her fingers. She was, all at once, entirely calm, in complete possession of herself. She stepped in front of the lifting automatic.

"Dick," she said urgently, "put down that gun before you hurt me. Dick, don't you know me?"

The gun was now pointing directly at Nita's breast. "I don't know you," Wentworth said woodenly. "Get out of the way."

Nita walked forward until the cruel steel of the automatic was gouging into her breast. "Dick," she whispered. "Look into my eyes, Dick, then say you don't know me."

Wentworth looked into her eyes and in his own there was no expression at all, no hint of recognition or of feeling.

"Get out of the way," he said, "so I can shoot that traitor."

"Get out of the way," Kirkpatrick echoed. "He won't shoot me!" His voice lacked confidence. Nita could tell that he was coming closer. Wentworth looked over her head and, abruptly, his face was convulsed with hatred. He caught Nita's shoulder in his left hand and tore her from in front of him. Nita had known he was strong, but she had never before felt his hostile strength. It was incredible, but that one hand upon her shoulder, dragging her aside, held her powerless. The fingers bit into the flesh so that a moan forced itself from her lips and she dropped on her knees.

She saw movement behind Wentworth and through the broken window came the bearded face of Ram Singh, drawn and wild-eyed.

"For God's sake," Nita gasped. "Stop him, stop him before it's too late. He has been hypnotized, Ram Singh! He's going to kill the Governor!"

Ram Singh had a leg over the window sill now and his black, fierce eyes jerked from person to person in the room.

Wentworth had his gun hand free, the weapon leveled at

Kirkpatrick. The Governor was too far away to reach him. If he moved it would precipitate the shot. His own gun was in his hand, but he would not use it. Wentworth's left hand held Nita motionless.

"Ram Singh," she cried. "Don't you understand. Wentworth *sahib* is hypnotized. If he kills his friend, he will kill himself when he understands. Stop him! Stop…!"

The pain of Dick's fingers on her shoulder choked off her voice. Dick was speaking, his voice harsh and unnatural. With an incredulous gasp, she realized that his voice held a strange accent, the accent of the Orient!

"Kirkpatrick," he cried. "You are a traitor to my Master, Wang-ba. Therefore, you die!"

HIS KNUCKLE whitened on the trigger. Nita gasped, squirmed against that imprisoning hand, but was helpless. Blackness floated before her eyes. Through the failing of her senses, she heard a shot and a blow, so intermingled that she could not tell which preceded the other. The fearful fingers relaxed from her shoulder and grayness swarmed about her.…

"Just a swoon," she heard some one say distantly. It sounded like Kirkpatrick, but Kirkpatrick was dead. She had heard the shot that killed him. Fingers massaged her throat, pressed strongly on the muscle cords of her nape. The grayness began to recede. Cold dampness of her temples knifed through her brain and she jerked up to a sitting position.

"Dick!" she cried. *"Dick!"*

She looked about frantically. Dick Wentworth lay on the floor beside her. There was blood on the side of his head. She was aware of guns crashing nearby and a hand touched her shoulder. She winced at the reminiscent pain.

"Keep down!" Kirkpatrick whispered. "They are attacking—" The crash of a shot drowned his voice—"attacking in force. But police are on the way. It won't be long."

"Dick!" she whispered. "But Dick...."

"Ram Singh knocked him out, that's all."

Nita's heart sprang up so suddenly, so joyfully that she almost choked. She got to her knees and groped about, found the automatic she had dropped. There should be five shots in it. She crouched beside Dick, smiling happily. She fired at a peaked head that showed in the window and the head disappeared. She laughed. With Dick free and on his trail, Wang-ba could not long prevail. She would cure Dick of his damnable drugs… She shot at a hand which looped over the window sill and a man screamed. Three shots left now!

Through the hammer of guns, she heard a shrill rising wail of police sirens; then there was another sound. It was a soughing, minor cry that seemed scarcely audible, yet rang painfully in her brain. She crouched, waiting with ready gun, but no more targets showed and the sirens waxed louder.

She began to laugh softly, thrust her knuckles in her mouth to stop the sound. It was over, all over. The men of Wang-ba were gone; police were here. It was over… The laughter beat her hand from her lips, tore at her throat. Kirkpatrick shook her.

"Stop that, Nita!" he said sharply. "Stop it. Hysterics! I'm ashamed of you, Nita!"

So that was what it was. Hysterics. Nita sucked in a deep

breath and got to her feet, breathed again. "All right," she said shakily. "I'm all right now."

When the police broke into the room, Ram Singh squatted down by Wentworth's side and stayed there, his eyes fierce on any man who moved toward them, his hand on his knife hilt. Nita saw that the Governor's secretary was curiously sprawled on the floor.

"Gas got him," Kirkpatrick said, his old clipped accents restored. "Would have got me, too, if you hadn't shouted to break the windows. There's something of Dick in you, Nita. You guess things, or know things, almost as intuitively as he. Only I think he would have shot that Chinese hand despite its message."

Nita nodded slowly. "I guess he would." She went toward Ram Singh. His face, looking up at her, held a stricken look.

"I hit him, *missie sahib*," he whispered. "I hit him, my master!" NITA NODDED and smiled with stiff lips. "It was the only thing to do, Ram Singh. He will tell you so when he is himself again." She stood frowning at the pain that would not leave the faithful Sikh's eyes.

"May Allah grant that you are right, *missie sahib*," he whispered. "Else this knife will pierce my heart... *missie sahib*, I failed my master. I could not follow the black motorboat last night and I went back to the car in time to see some one drive it away. I do not know now why I did not stop him, but I followed instead. The Daimler is parked in the street here now. When it stopped there, I heard shooting and came as quickly as I could. I came in time... to hit my master."

Nita dropped on her knees and touched Wentworth's forehead with soft, long fingers. If Kirkpatrick was making explanations to the police, she did not hear him. Gently, in the way that Dick had taught her, she lifted his eyelid, felt the pulse in his throat. A coldness raced up her arm. What she discovered was no result of the blow Ram Singh had struck, she suddenly knew, but of the machinations of Wang-ba. She fought down the rise of a new hysteria. Her hands knotted whitely.

"Ram Singh," she said, her voice harsh despite her efforts. "This is the third stage of hypnosis, the sleep. If he is not revived from it, he will die. Ram Singh, you are of the East, can you…? Can you…?"

"You mean, *missie sahib*, that it was not my blow, but…?"

"But the power of the Turtle, Ram Singh!"

Ram Singh swayed a little, squatting on his heels there on the floor of the shattered room. His eyes held a far-away look that robbed them of their fierceness. They were a little frightened. "I was in Tibet, *missie sahib*," he whispered. "In Tibet with the *sahib*. There is a way, but if it fails… if it fails, *my master dies!*"

"You will not fail, Ram Singh," Nita said, more calmly than she knew. "You will not fail, you *can not!*"

"I can not fail," Ram Singh's words were a litany. He repeated them in a muted chant. He came to his feet and stood looking down at Wentworth. His hands knotted into fists at his sides. Nita stood also and if her heart beat hollowly and with pain, her face was calm. She turned toward Kirkpatrick.

"Please, Stanley," she said in a dull voice, "can you clear the room? Dick—Dick's life is at stake."

Kirkpatrick whirled toward her. "His life!"

Nita explained rapidly. "Then we must get a doctor, a special-
ist at once!"

Kirkpatrick cried. "Inspector…"

"No, no, Stanley," Nita urged. "Not that. No doctor knows.
This is an illness of the brain, of the *will*. It is for Ram Singh
and me…." She turned away and presently heard Kirkpatrick
brusquely clear the room. He came to her side then and stared
down at the inert body of his friend.

"Can I help, Nita?"

"No, only go, Stanley, so we can begin."

The door closed softly behind him. Nita went down on her
knees, her hands clasped, her eyes lifted toward the shadowing
ceiling. An illness of will… and her weapon against death was
only love. She closed her eyes and filled herself with her weapon,
filled herself with love.

Above her head, Ram Singh muttered a harsh and resonant
phrase of a dialect she did not know, she whom Dick had taught
so many. A shudder raced over her. *Oh, God, Dick must not die…!*

CHAPTER 7
HAND OF DEATH

NITA OPENED her eyes and turned toward Ram
Singh. The bearded Sikh, who had never quailed before
an enemy, was trembling. His cheeks, above the black bush of
his beard, held a greenish cast. A great panic set Nita's heart to
fluttering. *Fear!* She knew it, too, but she must not let this man
upon whom so much depended recognize that fact. The East

was old in the ways of the occult, of the mind and its dominion over matter. There was no one else to whom she could turn, no one else who would give as selflessly of his very soul.

She said, very calmly. "Your will is a knife, Oh Ram Singh. Wield it for your master."

A convulsive shudder jerked at Ram Singh's shoulders, then he stood still and slowly his head lifted. A pride and a dignity touched him.

"I cannot fail!" he cried, the voice muffled in his chest. He, too, dropped on his knees beside Wentworth. In harsh Hindustani, he told Nita what was necessary. His conception of what had happened in far Tibet was colored by the demonology of a world which still slumbers in black ignorance, of a thousand tribes and conflicting theisms. To him, what he did was black magic, but Nita saw that there were great basic psychological truths beneath the form and the ritual.

"Demons," Ram Singh whispered, "have stolen the master's soul and carried it away to Wang-ba, to whom they owe allegiance. If we could kill Wang-ba, we could reclaim his soul, but we cannot. Neither can we overcome the demons for we cannot reach them. But *sahib* can reclaim his own soul. His soul is stronger than a thousand demons. We must arouse his soul, which they have drugged to sleep."

"How can we do that, Ram Singh?" Nita asked quietly, understanding that it was Wentworth's will they must arouse, the will that was strong enough to revive an almost dead man. The will to live. Doctors could cure almost anything when that will was fierce enough, but if the patient did not wish to live… It was that which they must awake in Wentworth, but how? How, since he slept this deep and dreamless sleep which was so close to death, which would end so soon in death if they did not intervene?

"Thy *karma* and his are one, *missie sahib,*" Ram Singh whispered. "You must reach him. Open his clothing there and put your hands upon his naked heart. Put thy mouth to his mouth. Look upon his eyes. You are one, thy *karma* is one. Reach into him with thy heart and thy will and thy soul."

Nita's hands trembled as they touched the heart of the man she loved. His lips were cold, cold and without response. A sickness crept through Nita but she drove it out with a sharp determination. She looked upon the closed eyes of Dick Wentworth.

"Breathe with him," Ram Singh whispered. "Let thy heart beat with his. Let thy body and thy soul know no rhythm that is not his."

A numbness crept over Nita, a heavy lethargy of will and physical being. When Ram Singh's hand closed on her shoulder she scarcely felt it.

"If you sleep," he cried. "*He* dies. Even as I said, thy karma is one. So easily do thy souls and bodies blend. Your will is his will. Presently, *missie sahib,* you must sleep, but when you sleep, it must be with the will to wake. My will shall fight for thine, my strength for thine. Is it understood, *missie sahib?*"

FROM THE depths of her lethargy—her deep rhythmic sense of sleep—Nita heard him and realized what he meant, realized that she had merged herself so surely, so closely with Dick that the lethargy of his will, of his spirit, had infected hers. She must continue that union, even into the depths of sleep.

Then she must struggle back from the blackness and drag his soul with hers. Incredible, and yet the very drowsy willessness that crept over her proved the truth of the thing she thought.

She thought, "I sleep, but I will awake. I sleep, but I will awake." And when she thought the word "I" she did not mean herself alone, she meant herself and this man who was hers so utterly that their very souls were one. She meant "We will awake." But the two were implicit in the one. It was beyond belief, but it was a fact.

"I sleep, but I will awake. I will. *I will!*"

She was aware of Ram Singh's hand upon her shoulder and it seemed that from his touch strength flowed into her body. Her hands spread upon Wentworth's chest, palms and fingers close, close. Her lips encompassed his and her breath came and went hissingly through her nostrils in a rhythm that was as slow as the sleeping breath of her lover. Her quick woman's heart slowed with her breathing....

"I sleep, but I will awake."

She was in impenetrable darkness that swirled and writhed like a living yet tangible thing. Out of that darkness, two points of black grew and grew until they had crowded out all the other blackness. Strange that blackness should show against blackness, but there was a flaming strength that crowded out all else... in those two points. Nita felt a greater, an overwhelming, lethargy. Death, it whispered, was a deeper, a more restful sleep. Only sink more deeply into these two living points of blackness....

"I will awake," something within Nita chanted. "I will awake!"

The points of blackness receded a little and she realized that they were eyes, *the eyes of Wang-ba!* Revulsion stirred within her, revulsion and her straining will. This was the enemy; Dick's enemy, her enemy. His eyes it was that commanded sleep, commanded death! Nita felt her will become a hard knot within her—a knot of pulsing strength. Wang-ba was trying to pull it out of her, to pull it out of her by her eyes. If she shut her eyes, it would make no difference. She began to fight to keep that knot of power within herself. There was a rhythmic chant within her that surely was not thought and was not will. It might be her blood that sang *"I will awake!"*

Those black eyes became even smaller and suddenly there was a snapping sound. Ah, the cord by which he sought to pull the knot from within her had broken. "I will awake, I will awake, I will, *will, WILL!*"

Nita opened her eyes and moved heavily, without strength. She moved her lips and other lips moved with them. The eyes into which she looked were not black, but blue-gray and suddenly they were smiling at her. She heard Ram Singh utter a great shout:

"He lives! My master lives!"

Nita felt arms tight about her, felt a kiss from those lips that had been so long motionless beneath hers. Heat that she knew was a blush washed up over her throat and cheeks and she pulled her lips from Dick's and buried her face in his chest. Above her head, she heard Dick's voice.

"What has happened, my brave one?" he said. "I remember being in a boat with Wang-ba and something struck me in the cheek."

"You were hypnotized, *sahib,*" Ram Singh said. "We have brought you back. The *missie sahib* has brought you back. Her karma is yours, master. You remember, Tibet...."

Wentworth's arms tightened about Nita's shoulders. "Tibet!" he cried. "Good God, Ram Singh, you might have killed her!" **NITA LIFTED** her face, grinned at Wentworth. "It will take more than a couple of black eyes telling me to kill myself to do it," she said, and then broke off and shuddered, remembering that darkness that had lived about her. Then she laughed. "By the heavens, Dick, you'll have to mind me hereafter. You certainly did... when those black eyes were on us."

Wentworth understood without words. There was still a great lassitude within him. He knew Nita's tiredness. He drove himself to his feet, lifted her, too, and stood with his arm about her.

"Why, good lord, this is Kirk's office in Pelham. The windows are broken," He turned frowning to Nita. "What happened, dear?"

Nita hesitated, then told him everything. He would have to know so that he would know how to fight the will of Wang-ba if the Chinese attempted to impose it upon him again. Wentworth's face paled a little as he realized what he had so nearly done. When Nita told him of Ram Singh's blow, he turned toward the Hindu and nodded.

"Thou art wise as well as brave, my warrior," he said. Ram Singh's bow, hands cupped to his forehead, was almost an obeisance. The door opened cautiously, then Kirkpatrick strode across with his hand outstretched.

90

"Glad to see you, Dick, old man," he said, his voice clipped and sharp to hide the emotion he felt. "Nita thought Ram Singh could do it...."

"Nita did it herself," Wentworth told him gravely. "I hope you are more glad to see me than last time we met."

Kirkpatrick's face went completely blank and Wentworth laughed. "Oh, I know everything, Kirk. No use your trying to hide it from me."

His face grew sober and his lips straightened and thinned. "This is our biggest fight, Kirk; our strongest enemy. I tell you the man is an absolute fiend!"

The Governor nodded, still clasping Wentworth's hand. "He plans to kill a thousand people tonight if we do not pay him a hundred million dollars."

"How?" Wentworth demanded.

Kirkpatrick shook his head, detailed the atrocities already contrived by Wang-ba, the burning of trains, the blowing up of the *Rex,* the gas. Wentworth lifted his hands to his head and pressed his temples. Nita watched him narrowly. She surmised that from now until Wang-ba died, Wentworth would be subject to the mental influence of the Chinese. She paled as she realized this meant that hers would probably be the hand that accomplished Wang-ba's death. The eyes of Wang-ba could check Wentworth in the very act of shooting him. It not only imperiled Dick, it made him an object of danger to his allies as well! Nita accepted the charge upon her with a slight straightening of her slim, shapely body.

Dick's hands swung down and he laughed. "Wang-ba slipped

up or else Nita did an uncommonly good job of nullifying his hypnotism. I remember… a great deal. His headquarters at present are aboard a submarine. Let airplanes search for him tomorrow, especially along the southern shore of Long Island and of New Jersey. There isn't water enough for his boat to get through the East River to the Sound. He could get into the Hudson, but the danger would be too great. He won't be there."

Kirkpatrick nodded, smiling a little with sheer relief at his friend's recovery.

Wentworth raced on. "We'll organize grenade patrols tonight," he said. "Use every available automobile and order everything except the patrols off the streets. All of the Chinese weapons ought to be subject to destruction by T.N.T.! We'll stand him off tonight, and tomorrow, the submarine…."

There was a hard, rapid pounding on the door and a police inspector burst in without waiting for permission. "My God, Governor!" he cried. "My God, Wang-ba has struck again. Hundreds are dead, hundreds! He says that because of treachery, he'll kill two thousand tonight. Tomorrow four thousand…."

Outside the window, there was a slight, scraping noise. Wentworth dived headlong against Kirkpatrick, swept him to the floor. Over their heads, something hissed and the police inspector screamed on a high, mad note.

Wentworth rolled over and over with Kirkpatrick, away from the policeman, away from any spot where they might be the target of a new attack. Across the office, the inspector was still screaming horribly and the room was flooded by a ghastly light. *The inspector was wrapped from head to foot in living flame!*

POLICE WHISTLES jabbered outside the Governor's mansion and men shouted in mad panic. There was more of that ghastly flame light outside and Wentworth, peering out of the window, saw three things that had been men racing in screaming circles, beating at fires that burned and burned. Of the assassin who had used this fearful weapon, there was no sign at all.

Wentworth straightened slowly and found Kirkpatrick standing, white-faced, beside him.

"Thanks, Dick," he said shakily. "I owe you my life once more."

Wentworth shrugged. "It might have been me they shot at," he said.

He turned to stare across the room. Ram Singh had wrapped the police inspector, unconscious now, in a rug snatched from the floor in an attempt to smother the flames, but even as Wentworth looked, green fire ate out through the rug and danced higher, higher. The ceiling mushroomed the blaze in all directions and the heat grew rapidly unbearable.

"Out the window!" Wentworth shouted. "Quickly, that fire spreads fast!"

Almost before Nita and the others could reach the windows, the flame was licking at the outer walls. Fire department sirens sounded eerily in the distance.

"I have a feeling," Wentworth said dully, "that nothing is going to extinguish those flames. Perhaps, they'll be able to keep them from spreading out of your office."

A police official hurried toward them. His jaw jutted belligerently. "Just like the fires in Manhattan," he said. "Half the West Side's in flames. Can't do a damned thing about it. Water spreads it. Burns without air, too, apparently. Can't smother it with extinguishers or anything else. Damned if I don't believe it would burn clean through the earth, given half a chance."

"Tell those firemen," Wentworth ordered sharply as a red engine screamed to a halt nearby and men ran for the water plugs with hose. "Tell them to put water curtains all around the room and wet the walls and floor above. Tell them to try small charges of dynamite, to blow it out."

Kirkpatrick stood grim-faced, unspeaking, beside him. This was the Governor's ancestral home. It had been in the family for over a hundred years and it was being destroyed before his eyes by deathless fires that nothing could extinguish.

"Hell fire," he whispered harshly. "Hell fire!"

Wentworth shook his head. "The only thing I know that behaves in this way is what the East calls 'elemental fire.' It's supposedly a thing generated by the will of a powerful mentality. It will consume bricks and stone walls as readily as wood. Not that I ever believed in it."

Kirkpatrick shrugged, turned to a State trooper standing nearby. "Tell them to save what furniture they can. I'm afraid the house is doomed. Dick, that looks like your car over there. Let's go to town."

Dick felt Nita's hand on his arm. "Dick, Wang-ba used your Daimler. A Chinese drove me to Stanley's New York headquarters in it, and now it turns up here."

Wentworth nodded. "Thanks, darling," he said. "We'd better use another car, Kirk, until experts can go over the Daimler for explosives and poisoned needles, hidden gas shells... Hell, better just blow it up and have done with it. I'll never feel safe in it again. For all I know, five years from now, some needles may work through the cushions and finish me off!"

"Don't blame you for feeling that way," Kirkpatrick nodded. "I'll have it searched, then stripped of upholstery and relined."

Wentworth smiled grimly. In a secret compartment there, police would find positive proof that Wentworth was the Spider. They would find guns with which the Spider had killed. They would find his clothing and the fine silken rope that served him wonderfully on more than one occasion.

"I won't let anyone take the risk," he said shortly. "Ram Singh, blow it up where it stands."

Ram Singh salaamed and marched off. Wentworth nodded. "One more score that Wang-ba will have to pay off."

They entered a police car and sped toward New York. Long before they reached the Harlem Ship Canal, they could see the red glow of a hundred fires blazing against the sky. Wentworth's long jaw set more firmly, his eyes were cold gleams of blue-gray ice. Not only had hundreds been killed this night, but they had died in inhuman torture, in the burning blanket of the deathless fires. Last night, it had been a poison gas of fearful potency. What would be the next torture weapon of Wang-ba? How and where would it strike?

Wentworth shook his head. There was no answer to those questions except in the headquarters of the Turtle! Wentworth knew that it would be useless for him to attempt to return to Wang-ba, pretending to be still under his hypnotic power. When Nita, descending in the vale of shadows to save him, had seen those black eyes, Wang-ba necessarily had been aware that some one was trying to break his influence over Wentworth. And he would be aware, too, that the effort had succeeded.

Through streets that still echoed to the wail of fire and ambulance sirens, the Governor's car rolled until it entered the automobile tunnels beneath the Waldorf-Astoria. Wentworth alighted with them and went to the Governor's suite. The chambers were crowded with officials of police and of the city government. They were frantic with fear. Even here, they cast uneasy glances at their neighbors. Kirkpatrick's arrival with Wentworth acted as a strong tonic. Chins lifted and eyes brightened....

In his private office, Kirkpatrick turned bitterly toward his friend. "You see, they expect miracles of me. It is in their eyes. And what can I do?"

Wentworth smiled slowly. "We will contrive the miracle."

He turned to Nita, drew her tenderly into his arms. "Stay here, sweetheart," he whispered. "Kirk can protect you more efficiently than I."

NITA READ his intention to leave her in his words and her hands clung to him, her eyes lifted in wordless appeal and he brushed their lids with his lips. She sighed and no longer clung. Within the hour, she had snatched him back from the brink of death, and already he was planning to plunge again into the maelstrom. It was useless to urge him to wait. She would not have him think her cowardly.

"I have to, sweetheart," he told her, reading her heart perfectly. "Kirk, I entrust Nita to you."

Kirkpatrick was standing with his long legs braced apart,

thumb and forefinger spreading his pointed mustache. There was a grim coldness about his eyes.

"Where are you going, Dick?" he demanded sharply.

Wentworth laughed. "If I could tell you, Kirk, I could lead you to the headquarters of Wang-ba! I'll communicate when I can." He clasped the Governor's hand tightly, looked again into Nita's eyes, then he strode toward the door, his shoulders swinging in their old confident way, his head lifted. Nita heard his voice, vibrant and vital, as he greeted some one in the ante-chamber; then he was gone. She turned toward Kirkpatrick, setting her lips hard against the tremble that was in them. So soon, so soon! Kirkpatrick dropped into his chair and pressed a button on his desk.

"I feel as if half my life had gone away," he told Nita dully. "God knows when and where we'll see him again."

"God knows," Nita repeated, quietly. She walked blindly to the window and looked out on the smoke-thickened night. The streets were nearly deserted. The terror of the Turtle was on the city. Police were hard at work, of course, but well she knew how futile their efforts would be. Against the ordinary run of criminals, they were tremendously effective. But against such mental monsters as Wang-ba, they had no weapons. One man stood between Western civilization and this peril out of the East—one man who carried her heart with him. She pressed her hands hard against her mouth.

Dimly, she could hear Kirkpatrick giving some instructions to his secretary, then the phone buzzed dimly. The Governor's voice sharpened. She turned and he was hanging up. He looked into her eyes.

"The Spider just called," be said. "He warned me not to let Dick come near me again—until Wang-ba was dead."

Nita caught her breath, then smiled. Kirkpatrick knew as well as she that Dick Wentworth and the Spider were one. It was a bitter and a proud moment for them both. Wentworth was guarding his friend against the subtleties of Wang-ba. Well he knew that he might again submit to that mighty mentality, and if that happened, he did not intend Kirkpatrick to suffer through their friendship.

It told Nita something else. Tonight, the Spider would be born again, the Spider whom Underworld and police alike would kill on sight even though the destiny of the Western world rested upon his proud shoulders!

CHAPTER 8
RETURN OF THE SPIDER

AFTER HE had made that bitter phone call to Kirkpat- rick, Wentworth returned to his penthouse apartment where he found the old butler waiting wearily for him. If Jenkyns had slept since his departure, it was in that old stiff-backed chair that stood in the hall. He gazed on Wentworth with affectionate eyes. "Have you slept, Master Dick?"

Wentworth laughed, shook his head. "Have you, Jenkyns?"

They laughed together. "Let me give you a rubdown, Master

Dick," Jenkyns urged. "I know you too well to urge that a full night's sleep...."

"Two hours, Jenkyns, two hours!" Wentworth was sober, grim-faced again. "It's eight now. By ten thirty at the latest, I must be on my way."

Jenkyns sighed his resignation and they repaired to Wentworth's sleeping quarters, a four-room suite, one room of which, adjoining the luxurious bath, was fitted with a padded table. On this Wentworth stretched his lean, tanned body while Jenkyns, with the skill of long practice, relaxed his taut, weary muscles with prodding, slapping hands.

Afterwards, Wentworth slept between silken sheets and two hours later, he bounded to his feet with his matchless energy fully restored. He bantered with Jenkyns as he swiftly ate and dressed. The eyes of the two men met and held when Wentworth strapped beneath his arms the holsters of his swift, deadly guns and appended to the left one the kit of tools which served the Spider so well. Jenkyns helped him into his smoothly fitted coat and, in the mirror, Wentworth glimpsed his worried old face. Jenkyns sighed.

"How long, Master Dick?" he faltered. "How long before you stop this madness and you and Miss Nita...?"

Wentworth's face went blank, his eyes tightened against pain. "Probably never," he cried, with affected gaiety. "Why, Jenkyns, what would you do if you didn't have me to worry about? You'd die of boredom."

"There might be another, younger Dick," Jenkyns said soberly, "to worry about. I'd like that much better."

Wentworth's hands closed at his sides, and his laughter seemed brittle and hard even in his own ears. He had seen that unspoken dream of babies in Nita's eyes, too.

"The black felt and cape, Jenkyns," he said harshly.

"Yes, Master Dick." There was a slump in the aged butler's shoulders as he walked away.

Wentworth glared at his own reflection in the mirror. Thoughts like these were madness, and he knew their result. He would be more reckless than ever when he entered battle, drowning out memories and hopes. God, but it was cruel to Nita, this life of his. Always, he hoped when he put down one more of these damnable madmen who sought to twist the world into their own megalomaniac kingdom, that it would be the last. And always some new fool... He shook his head. Nita had entered his life with a full knowledge of what lay ahead. She never had complained, but hope died hard....

HE SNATCHED the broad-brimmed hat from Jenkyns, flung the cape savagely about his shoulders and strode toward the service elevator. The superintendent of the building was used to seeing many strange men come and go through the secret entrance in the basement. He thought that Wentworth did a great deal of secret police work, that the strange seeming men who came and went were spies. How could he know that it was only one man, Wentworth, in disguise? Besides, Wentworth owned the building. It was not for him to question.

As the automatic elevator stopped and Wentworth opened the door, Jenkyns behind him quavered, "Good night, Master Dick."

"A friend!" he cried. "I am a friend from Wang-ba!"

Wentworth jerked about and stared at him. In a single long stride, he had reached Jenkyns and clasped the man's hand.

"It's all right, Jenkyns," he said, "but for God's sake, don't do it any more. Do you want to turn me into a coward?"

Jenkyns laughed ruefully as Wentworth strode back to the elevator. "I wish that I might, Master Dick, but I'm afraid there's no use hoping...."

Wentworth was smiling slightly as the elevator went swiftly downward. He was thinking that he was singularly unworthy of such devoted friends and servants, Jenkyns and Jackson and Ram Singh, Nita and Kirkpatrick... He drew in a sharp, quavering breath. Tomorrow, he must go to see Jackson and try to pull him out of the madness into which Wang-ba had thrown him... He shook his head sharply, closed his mind on such weakening thoughts. He had one purpose in life now—the death of Wang-ba. It must not be long delayed!

IN THE morning, airplanes would seek for the submarine. Even if they found it, destroyed it with bombs, he had small hope that the Turtle would be upon it. The man would realize that with the failure of his plan to seize Kirkpatrick would come the revelation by Wentworth and Nita of his hideout on the water. No, no, it was up to the Spider to find and destroy the man.

Wentworth's lips twisted at the thought. But would he, when the time came, be able to fire the fatal shot? He would never know until the crisis was at hand. How far had he succumbed to the will of the monster? Wentworth's hand rose unconsciously to his cheek, touched the minute wound there through which the drug had entered his body. There was a hint of grim laughter in his eyes. That drugged dart had been in itself a confession of weakness. Wang-ba had seen death in Wentworth's eyes, in the gun that rose despite his most strenuous exertion of will, and he had signaled his underling to fire the narcotic dart.

With a start, Wentworth remembered the shot that had been fired as he himself had fallen and he knew suddenly what that shot had been. Wang-ba had killed the man who fired the dart, because that man had seen his will overcome! Wentworth laughed softly to himself, and a resolution formed in his mind. When the end came, he would face Wang-ba in his own person-ality, and he would vanquish him in a duel of wills! Vanity, Went-worth assured himself. He was giving way to personal pride, but he knew that just such an outcome was necessary if he were to preserve his own faith in himself—the utter self-confidence which alone had carried him victorious through a thousand encounters with death....

Wentworth looked about him at the dark and deserted streets. It was still early in the evening, but there was no traffic except the cars of the military carrying armed men. Grenade patrols. Kirkpatrick had already put his suggestion into operation. Well, it would hamper the Spider, but that was unimportant beside the difficulties it would place in the way of Wang-ba. If the Spider failed to find the Chinese, the city must be guarded against the terror promised for the next night when four thousand persons were to die!

There was another danger which the people at large had not yet begun to realize. Food supplies were dwindling. With water and train routes blocked by the minions of Wang-ba, with the highways menaced by strange and horrible weapons of destruction, outside help was entirely cut off. Day after tomorrow, at the latest, the pinch of hunger would begin to add to the suffering. Absolute panic would reign. Day after tomorrow, at the latest, Kirkpatrick would be forced to arrange to comply with the demands of Wang-ba. A hundred million dollars for the release of New York City—and no guarantee that the monster would not immediately demand a larger ransom, that he would not once more loose his destroying powers upon the people to force the payment. Wentworth did not for a moment suppose that the Chinese would be so easily satisfied. Undoubtedly, his ambitions would dictate continued dominion over these easily mulcted people of the West.

There was, Wentworth realized, one sure way of establishing contact with Wang-ba. If he were to try to bring in one of the trains of food supplies with which railroad lines were loaded no farther away than Poughkeepsie, he would immediately challenge the Chinese to strike. Wentworth did not doubt that Wang-ba would eagerly snatch up the gage of battle! The Spider's hands touched the guns beneath his arms. Feeble weapons with which to brave the terror of Wang-ba, but they would serve!

WENTWORTH MADE his way speedily to the Floyd Bennett airport and a half hour later was landed at Poughkeepsie. He had traveled under his own identity, but now he slipped into a railway waiting-room lavatory and took out a compact make-up kit from an inner pocket of the black cape. Before the cracked and discolored mirror, he went swiftly to work upon his face.

The skin of his cheeks tautened and became sallow, shiny where it stretched over bones. There was the slightest of upward turn to his eye corners and his nose was quickly built into a predatory beak. His lips vanished entirely, his mouth was a straight, ominous line. That was all except for bushy, thick brows and a wig of long, lank hair. But when it was finished the face that stared back at Wentworth was a menacing, portentous thing. He dragged the slouch hat far down on his brows and the cape, upon his shoulders, was no longer smooth fitting and faultless. The back was hunched as if by a malignant deformity. When he walked, it was with a slight limp. Here was a figure from which the world of evil cringed as from the phantom of Death itself. Here was… the Spider!

Wentworth drew his cape close about him and, as silent and inconspicuous as a shadow, he stole into the darkness.

In an office building, a half-dozen blocks away, officials of the New York Central Railway sat in conference. The executive vice-president, Harry Malloy, was hunched over a desk, his bald, hair-fringed head, thrust forward with determination. He was in his shirt-sleeves and the garish light of an unshaded bulb glinted on sleeve-garters of baby-blue, fastened with gold. Malloy had come up from the ranks and he was a fighter.

"We're going through," he told the other four men with him. "By God we're going through if every Chinese in North America is out there trying to stop us."

The traffic manager had kept his coat on. He had a sharp,

thin-nosed face. Pince-nez glasses were balanced delicately before washed-out blue eyes.

"You can't," he pointed out precisely, "run the trains, for instance, if there are no tracks. You haven't forgotten what happened to the last train?"

Malloy hadn't forgotten and a bull-like rumble was deep in his solid throat at the memory. Flames had sprung from nowhere and engulfed engine and cars. Nothing except twisted heaps of iron junk had survived and those had only just been cleared away by the wreckers.

"The damages,"—Traffic-Director Denson pointed out, his thin voice like his face, sharp and precise—"the damages for delay will be considerably less than the cost of train after train being destroyed through your bullheadedness. Don't forget the pensions that are going to be paid to the widows of men who die."

Malloy's big fist made the articles on his desk jump. "New York is starving," he thundered, "and you talk of money!"

Denson's face flushed slightly, spots of color on the sharp cheek-bones. "Unfortunately," he said smoothly, "railroads are run to make money—or so I have been told!"

Malloy came slowly to his feet, hands pressing down hard on the desk, the hump of his shoulders large behind his bald head.

"The train is going through!" he shouted.

Behind him, a shade flapped up to the ceiling. A mocking, light voice said, "Bravo, Malloy. Bravo!"

Malloy whirled about and Denson whipped excitedly to his feet. None of the other men moved. The figure in the window was hunch-backed, sinister with the swing of his black cape about him. The face was keen, but menacing. Denson's voice broke into a thin squeal.

"The Spider! The Spider!" he gabbled.

The awkward figure in the window swept a neat bow. "Precisely, Denson," he said. "I am the one who will take your train through into New York City. At your service, Malloy."

MALLOY CAME out of his crouch, but his manner remained belligerent as he glared at the Spider.

"You're a crook," he growled. "I want nothing to do with you."

The Spider laughed at him. "Some other time, we'll dispute the matter, Malloy, but just now the important thing is to get food to New York. You agree with that?"

"Suppose I do?"

Wentworth nodded. He liked the fighting nature of the man as much as he detested the quibbling of Denson. He knew both of them personally, had fought with them over director's tables.

"I have a plan," he said equably. "Send a string of empties toward the city. I'll ride ahead of it on a gasoline car and I'll guarantee that your food train, following at a discreet distance, will have a clear path."

"How can you?" Malloy demanded.

Wentworth laughed. "It would take too long to tell you, Malloy. *Stand still, Denson. Sit down, you others!*" Wentworth's voice turned abruptly cold and brittle and his eyes flashed toward the men who had moved secretly toward the door. "I know there's fifty thousand dollars reward out for me, but none of you is going to collect it." The Spider did not have a gun in his hand, but the men obeyed with faces that were drained with fear. The Spider's swift ability to kill, his mercilessness were well known throughout the breadth of the Land. They did not stop to think that he had never harmed an innocent man....

"How about it, Malloy?" Wentworth challenged. "You say you want to get food through to New York. I tell you that I can show you the way. Do you hesitate?"

"I'd like to know how?" Malloy demanded stubbornly.

Impatience welled up within Wentworth. It flashed coldly from his eyes and he saw that Denson shrank and half-lifted trembling hands before his face.

"You'll have to take me on trust," the Spider snapped. "Come, man, you know my reputation. You know what I have done against criminals. How long will you hesitate?"

Malloy's face showed a grudging respect. He was a fighter himself, and he had admired this fighting man who called himself the Spider. He felt a rush of friendliness. After all, for the time being, they were on the same side of the fence.

"It's worth my job if we fail," he said dryly. "You can't blame me for hesitating. There's Denson, of course, to consider."

The Spider's lips parted in a thin smile. "I'll take care of Denson," he said shortly.

Malloy said, "Thanks, I can handle him." He spun about. "Assemble a food cargo at once, two food trains of miscellaneous stuff. If one can get through, two can. Get a short string of empties ready, too, and the fastest gasoline car."

Denson could face Malloy, though he had shrunk from the direct cold glare of the Spider. "I shall execute your orders, of course," he said dryly, "but you can't expect me not to make a report about this to the board of directors."

"Report, and be damned to you!" Malloy shouted. "Get moving! I'm going with you on the gasoline car, Spider," he said, his voice daring Wentworth to deny him.

"You've a very good chance of not coming out alive," the Spider warned him. He saw Malloy's anger mount and smiled slightly. "Very well, if you wish to run the risk, I don't know why I should try to stop you. There'll be work for both of us. You start out on the gasoline car; I'll join you later."

WENTWORTH MOVED toward the window and Malloy took a step after him. He was frowning and suspicious. "What's the idea?" he demanded.

Wentworth's eyes flashed toward Denson, toward the other men in the room. "Fifty thousand dollars is a lot of money," he said, gently, then he ducked out of the window and was gone. Malloy, when he reached the window seconds later, could see nothing of the Spider. He didn't look sideways along the building to the window, three offices away, to which Wentworth had swung like a pendulum at the end of a length of silken rope that dangled from the roof.

The Spider, making his way swiftly downstairs to the street, was frowning slightly. He had given Malloy the impression that he had a way of getting the food trains through. Actually, nothing of the sort was the case. He merely planned to form contact with the men of Wang-ba. Once that was done, he hoped to be able to eliminate them—to drive them in defeat back to some headquarters of the Turtle. Following them, he might reach

Wang-ba himself. It was simple, but in Wentworth's experience, most plans that succeeded had simplicity.

The police attempt to trap him which he more than half expected failed to materialize and he guessed that he had Malloy to thank for that. Wentworth secreted himself in the shadows of the tiny gasoline car's cab that he saw put on the tracks and waited there for over a half hour while Malloy got the trains organized. Presently, Malloy's big-shouldered figure loomed out of the darkness and climbed into the car.

"Quiet, Malloy," Wentworth whispered. "I'm already aboard."

Malloy said nothing until after he had the gasoline car under way, then he twisted his head about with a grin on his wide, fighter's face.

"I made those two-timing eggs come with us," he said, "Denson and the others. They're in a pilot train that will run right behind us, just a locomotive and a single car, full of armed men."

Wentworth shook his head. "I'm afraid you're taking them to their death," he said slowly. "They aren't at all necessary."

Malloy grunted. "Can't see two men taking a train through that yellow devil's blockade, but maybe you can."

Wentworth shrugged mentally. The armed men might help, but he was not depending on them. He picked up a rifle from the seat. It was one of the new type scheduled to be used if ever the United States army went to war again. Smaller caliber than the old Springfield, but higher velocity; a semi-automatic arm that carried ten bullets in the magazine and ejected and loaded automatically.

"If you'll turn on your dash-light," he told Malloy steadily, "you'll find a map of the railroad. I've marked six points of maximum danger, based on your two previous wrecks. Both of them occurred at points where the tracks swing very close to the river, and where also there are facilities for landing. Wang-ba operates from the water."

Malloy's grunt was less skeptical than previously. "Sounds good. What do you want to do when we reach those points? Speed up?"

"No," Wentworth corrected. "Slow down. I want to be able to see what I shoot at."

MALLOY CHUCKLED. "I brought a six-shooter," he jerked over his shoulder. He had the gasoline car running to his satisfaction now and turned from watching the rails to look narrow-eyed at the Spider. "I never thought I'd tie up with you, Spider," he said. "Thought more than once I'd have a crack at that reward just for the fun of it. You wouldn't kill me, you know."

Wentworth laughed, but made no other answer. No use quarreling with Malloy. There would be deadly work for both before long. He was checking his two heavy automatics which, as usual, were in perfect order. He dragged a heavy box out from under the single seat in the cabin of the gas-car, ripped it open.

"Grenades!" he said. "Good. They're useful, but they may blow us up."

Malloy just stood looking at him. Presently, he nodded his big head. "You'll do, Spider," he said. "I can see that face of yours is a fake, but I like your eyes." He turned briskly back to the map.

If he feared the uneven odds ahead, he gave no sign. "About two miles to that first danger point."

"Might as well slow down right away," Wentworth cautioned. "Five miles an hour is plenty fast. Will the pilot keep clear?"

Malloy grunted and the motor spluttered to a slower tempo; the car's speed dwindled. The sky was clear, there was no moon, but a faint gleam from the stars touched the rails ahead with silver. It seemed as incongruous as a butterfly sipping blood. Death was somewhere near, if not at this point, where the rails rode a high embankment that sloped away to broken rocks and the river, then at some other of the six points Wentworth had marked. Would Wang-ba use his Deathless Fires again? A single shell in the cabin of this car would doom both himself and Malloy beyond hope. Those flames would eat straight through living flesh. Wentworth's jaw hardened.

Seconds dragged past with the slow clicking of the rail joints beneath them and the river began to wind away from the right of way. Wentworth's eyes ceaselessly scanned the rocks to each side. Five minutes dribbled by. The speed of the car picked up. Wentworth let out a slow, long breath between his teeth and realized that his forearms ached from gripping his guns.

"Number one," he said, metallically.

Malloy nodded. His shoulders seemed swollen as he humped forward over the controls.

"I hope we get one crack at them before the fire gets us," he muttered.

More miles rolled under the wheels and presently it was time to cut speed again. Malloy's hand seemed reluctant as it moved the throttle. "We're sure giving them every chance to pot us."

"Yes," Wentworth agreed. "Will the pilot train blow at every place I've marked without signal?"

Malloy glanced at the chart. "Should," he said. "There's crossings and curves and things…."

Behind them, the locomotive whistle broke into a throaty wail. Wentworth's muscles tightened and he half-lifted his guns. Was he mistaken, or had there been a faint, greenish glare against the sky just ahead where tracks slashed through a hillside? He could tell from the rigid set of Malloy's shoulders that he had glimpsed the same thing. It seemed crazy, suicidal, to charge into the flaming death at this slow pace.

"What do you think, Malloy?" Wentworth asked softly.

"Damned good place for it," Malloy grunted. "The cut's deep. Thick trees at the top of the banks. Plenty of rocks. They could just drip fire down on us. A cove beyond with gradual banks."

The gasoline car was almost in the shadow of the cut. Abruptly, Wentworth cried, "Go through fast."

"What's the matter, son, lose your nerve?" Malloy jeered, but he speeded up the car.

"We'll cover the cove," Wentworth told him shortly, his anger rising. "Flash light signals to the pilot train to attack from the other side. I don't suppose you told them back there to watch for signals?"

Malloy laughed harshly. "I was in the war, son. We learned about keeping contact over there."

WENTWORTH CALMED himself with an effort. Their

brittleness of temper was a reflection of the tension under which they worked. The gasoline car was sputtering along at between thirty and thirty five miles an hour, its top speed. Wentworth stood in the right hand door with automatics in his fists. Nothing happened. At the end of the cut, Malloy dragged on brakes and brought the car to a halt. A grenade in each fist, his automatics holstered, Wentworth stepped out on the flat platform at the back of the car.

"What's your best distance with the grenade?" he asked lightly.

"About seventy-five yards," Malloy's voice was flat. "Maybe eighty."

"Let's clear the car of all weapons," Wentworth said, "and try a couple of bombs on each side of the cut. Just to make sure."

Malloy grunted and heaved the grenade box to the side of the track, dragged it off into the bushes, came back with one in each fist. He squinted at the embankments to right and left of the cut.

"I can just about reach that big rock there."

"Okay," Wentworth agreed. "I'll take the pine tree there on the opposite side. Ready? One—two—*three....*"

The grenades arched through the air, vanished into the night; then white-and-red flame blasted the darkness out of existence. Mingled with the explosion, came the shrill, wailing scream of a man. Wentworth cried out in triumph and leaped for the side of the tracks, with Malloy just behind him. They were not a moment too soon. With a hissing warning, some missile swished through the night and burst with a thin tinkle against the gasoline car. A moment of silence then, and green flames began to lick upward. They grew by prodigious leaps and the two men crept deeper into the underbrush, heard the crackle and hiss of the Deathless Fire of Wang-ba.

Wentworth caught hold of Malloy's arm. "This is as far as I go," he said sharply. "I'm going down to the cove so that I can trail the devils when they pull out. This is probably the only ambuscade, but if there are others a foray on foot in advance of the train should eliminate them."

Malloy turned toward him. In the green glare of the flames, his face was set and hard. "We'll get the trains through now, thanks to you." His hand shot out abruptly to grasp Wentworth's. "Luck, Spider. Wish I was going with you. Don't mind my grousing back there."

Wentworth smiled. For a moment, he wished the man could go with him, too. He was brave, competent. When it came to a final show-down with Wang-ba, Malloy could kill him if the Spider's will faltered under the mental assault of the Chinese. The smile hardened. That was the Spider's task. He would perform it. He wrung Malloy's hand, and was gone into the darkness. As he crept down the slope he heard another grenade burst with a vicious concussion.

The first step of his simple plan had succeeded, but from now on, the way was much more perilous. If there were a boat in the cove, he must get aboard it and remain concealed. Failing that, he must allow himself to be taken, a prisoner, to Wang-ba. Malloy would get through. It was always easy to follow when some one else had shown the way....

Wentworth pushed through the shrubbery and spied down on

the glinting surface of the water. It was unbroken. No boat rested there. The devil! Had he made a mistake then? He abruptly recalled the Chinese chained to the steam roller. Would these men also die at their posts rather than flee back to Wang-ba?

The Spider faced about. There was only one thing for him to do, then. He must go up there where the grenades were bursting—where soon the railway men would attack—and make sure that one of the Chinese risked return to Wang-ba!

CHAPTER 9
FETTERS OF FLAME

A S WENTWORTH made his way swiftly through the bushes toward the crest of the rise where the Chinese had their flame-throwing fortress, he saw a powerful flashlight begin to wink at the sky. Malloy was signaling the men on the pilot train. Almost instantly, the whistle of the locomotive blasted a series of short and long notes into the night.

Within minutes, the armed men from the train would deploy on each side of the track and rake through the woods for the Chinese, wipe them off the face of the earth. Yes, it certainly looked as if the food trains would get through to New York… Wentworth was within thirty yards of the spot from which the Chinese had fired. He could identify it by the tall pine at which he had aimed his grenades. It was leaning a little now, its roots weakened by the explosions.

Wentworth was remembering the previous occasion when the hellions of Wang-ba had been called off by a moaning wail

116

that died out through the minor keys. If he could duplicate that… He threw back his head, cupped his mouth with one hand and sent a cry through the night. Wentworth was a musician, He had the gift of absolute pitch, and the cry was a perfect imitation. He waited to see the results of his retreat signal. Nothing happened at all. He could hear Chinese voices gabbling in sing-song, but they remained stationary. They were burdened with fright.

Something thumped to the ground ten yards away and Wentworth flung himself prone just in time. Fragments of a bursting grenade screamed over his head. He let out an anguished scream and afterwards his lips set in a thin smile. It would be well if he did not forget Malloy's grenades again. He wriggled rapidly forward, heard a second grenade thud behind him. The concussion half-stunned him. He shook his head and crawled on.

The Chinese could not be far ahead now, but they would be as anxious to kill him as Malloy with his damnable accuracy. He could hear the calls of the railroad men as they spread out on both sides of the right-of-way. Whatever he did must be done quickly, or it would be to late… He flung to his feet and raced forward, shouting phrases in Chinese….

"A friend!" he cried. "I am a friend from Wang-ba!"

A moment later, he was in the midst of a half-dozen Chinese. One lay terribly torn at the foot of the leaning pine, having taken the full force of a grenade. The others squatted on their heels. They were equipped with cross-bows of the ancient Genoese type and beside each man was a thicket of cross-bolts whose tips were little glass tubes. So this was how the Deathless Fire was hurled…!

"You must run away," Wentworth cried at them. "Me come from Head Man. You run away chop chop!"

Then he saw what he had half-expected to find. Each man was chained fast to a heavy stone, fastened there hopelessly to battle until he died. He saw something else. In each chain was a link of hollow glass and with horror in his eyes, he realized that this also must contain the fearful liquid of the Deathless Fires!

WENTWORTH BENT over the chain of the nearest man, and the fellow screamed in an agony of fear, chattering in a strange dialect with which Wentworth was unfamiliar. He gathered that if the glass broke, the flame would be thrown on the unfortunate to which the chain was fastened—that there was no escape from the Devil Flame. Wentworth's lips twisted with the memory of what Kirkpatrick had called this same substance, so close to the Chinese phrase. Hell fire, he had said. Hell fire….

A grenade burst a dozen yards down the slope and from the opposite direction came the trampling of underbrush where the men advanced. One of the Chinese whipped up his cross-bow and sent a bolt hurtling through the darkness. There was a burst of greenish flame that instantly leaped high into the air. The underbrush crackled and broke into blaze and men screamed. The fire spread rapidly. Evidently, the victory was not to be as easy as he had expected. These men had chains for morale. They could not retreat….

A withering blast of gun-fire racketed up from the shrubbery. The bullets flew high, or plowed through the earth at the brow of the hill, whined off rocks. One whimpered past Wentworth's ear and he squatted down. It would help no one if he were to be killed here! His hand went rapidly to the compact tool kit beneath his arm and drew out a slender lock-pick of surgical steel. He set to work on the anklet of the nearest Chinese and almost instantly it yielded to his skill.

"Wait," he ordered the liberated Chinaman and went to the next man.

With a sinking heart, Wentworth realized that he could not hope to stop the Chinese from firing at the men who advanced upon them. If he did, they would no longer trust him, or believe that he came from Wang-ba. And it was desperately necessary that they do so. He had no other means of reaching the headquarters of the Turtle. One thing he could do. He could hurry the work upon the men's shackles. Two, three, four men he freed and they cowered to the ground, waiting for his orders. They kept up no persistent fire upon the railway men, but now and again, a new burst of the Devil Flame would spring up out there in the brush. One man, a living tower of fire, ran screaming up the railroad tracks until he fell between the rails and lay there burning, his cries hushed at last.

Wentworth's hands seemed weighted with lead and yet they moved swiftly about his task while he bent over the fifth man. As he labored frantically to free this last man, a grenade, hurled this time by the railway men, burst not twenty feet away and, without a sound, the man on whom he worked flopped backward to the earth. In his dying convulsions, he snapped the glass link of the chain and instantly a spurt of green fire sprang up from his body.

Wentworth leaped backward with a choked cry, barely avoiding the fearful stuff. From the underbrush came a new, hammering outburst of gun-fire and he flung himself to earth and wriggled toward the other Chinese.

"Come along!" he shouted at them and led the way toward the cove. It was obvious that the Chinese had been left no means of escape, otherwise they would not have been chained to their stations upon the railroad. He frowned, remembering the green flash across the sky which he and Malloy had seen. Surely, some sort of signal....

Back on the hill, he heard the burst of two grenades in quick succession and instantly there was an incredible green glare leaping to the sky. The missiles of the Chinese, left behind, had been smashed. Even a hundred yards away, slipping rapidly through the brush, Wentworth felt the heat of the Devil Flame. Trees sprang instantaneously into blaze, and the crackling of the fire drowned out all other sound. The green light died and Wentworth ran on....

He had almost reached the sands of the cove when he saw a heavy, wide-shouldered man step out of the shrubbery and poise a grenade on his palm. Malloy! There could be no mistaking his heavy, powerful figure. But, damn it, the man was jeopardizing an entire city by his blood-thirsty determination to wipe out the Chinese!

Wentworth's hand flew to his holster even as the grenade arched through the air. His teeth set fiercely. He could barely see the bomb, tumbling lazily toward them in the darkness. If it landed near them... Wentworth's automatic spat spiteful flame upward into the night, missed. Missed again! Even the Spider's unerring accuracy was strained to the utmost by that half-seen, moving target. His third bullet detonated the grenade while it was still high in the air. The concussion was fearful. Fragments spat at the earth and one Chinese, two paces from Wentworth's side, screamed as steel tore through his flesh.

Malloy was balancing another grenade on his palm, his two hands met together to yank the pin. Wentworth's gun was a living, sentient thing that acted of its own accord. He could not miss. The bullet smashed Malloy's wrist, whirled him about and dropped him to the ground. Instantly, Wentworth was on his feet, racing forward. It was forty yards and, if Malloy had yanked the pin, there was small hope that the Spider could reach there in time to save him before the grenade exploded.

If, however, the pin had only been pulled as he fell, there was a chance, a bare chance. The grenades had five-second fuses. Wentworth had sprung forward even as he fired, and he was a champion sprinter. Four seconds and a fifth, maybe two… Malloy was on his feet now, groping for the right side of his trousers with his left hand, going for his six-shooter. The damned fool! He must have gone berserk with battle rage!

Wentworth's head was flung back, his legs pistoned, spurning the wet sand of the beach. "The grenade!" he gasped. "Throw the grenade into the water!"

Malloy caught his meaning and swung about, staggering as he turned, standing on wide-spraddled legs to maintain his balance. It was apparent that he was still dazed by the shock of his wound. While he ran, Wentworth's keen eyes searched the white sand for the grenade. He saw it, almost on the water's brink and a gasp of relief pushed into his throat. It had been thrown almost ten yards toward him when the bullet struck Malloy's wrist. That gave him a little more time, split-seconds more.

WITH SOMETHING like a curse, he slid to a halt beside the bomb and caught it with both hands, snatching it up and throwing it far out into the water with the same movement. It struck with a splash that instantly became a geyser as the thing exploded. Malloy was bending over the grenade box for another bomb. Wentworth whirled toward him, covered the distance that separated them in two long strides. His fist caught Malloy's jaw and knocked him backward into the bushes. He lay where he had fallen.

Up on the right-of-way, a rifle cracked and the lead skipped away across the surface of the river. Wentworth turned and, with a shout to the Chinese to follow, dived into the cove. He curved instantly to the surface and saw three heads bobbing behind him. He struck out straight across the Hudson River, slightly under a half-mile wide at this point.

Could the Chinese make it? He had no way of telling, but at least they had followed him into the water without hesitation. One of them *must* survive! He pushed on with a slow and steady stroke. He thought with a grimace of disgust that his guns would probably be fouled by the water. His holsters were lined with rubber and the working parts of the gun fitted snugly into them against such emergencies as this, but it was a chance—a chance he would have to take. He kept a keen eye on the three Chinese as he pushed forward. So far they were swimming well.

He could see the shadows of men on the beach, against the leaping glare of the fire that was spreading rapidly through the underbrush. Its light shone far out on the water, too, and already four men with rifles were blazing away at their bobbing heads. They would make difficult targets, Wentworth knew, but it would be better to minimize the chances of a hit as much as possible. He shouted to the men to swim under water and set them an example. Lead cut the water near his head as he ducked under....

When Wentworth's feet finally touched the far shore and he crawled toward the shrubbery, only two men were with him. One of them gasped out a bullet had "finished along Li-Chiu altogether!" At least they had the width of the river between them and the railway men. They could take more time about finding a boat.

The November air was chill. Wentworth's teeth chattered a little. He set a brisk pace that was half-run and they moved rapidly along through the edge of the trees that marched down near the water. They would make a poor target for the vengeful rifles if they could be seen at all. They had to travel a mile before they found a motorboat. At a sign from Wentworth, one of the Chinese plunged into the water again and drew the craft to shore. It took a half hour to free it of its padlock and to rewire the ignition. Once it was under way, Wentworth turned over the wheel to one of the Chinese and set about finding dry clothing in the lockers.

He needed the clothing, heaven knew, but that was only an excuse. By turning over the wheel to the Chinese, he avoided the revelation that he did not know where to steer the boat. And the Chinese, by the competent manner in which he took hold, showed that he *did* know! At last, the Spider was on his way toward the lair of the Turtle!

IT WAS characteristic of the Spider that he thought with a transcendent joy of his coming invasion of the Turtle's head-quarters. It was not that he underestimated his enemy or that he did not know that death would surround him in a thousand eerie forms once he entered the place. But it was a goal he had set himself. It was near achievement, and he had considered the dangers in advance....

He had carried out two, no three, steps of his plan. He had done better than follow the Chinese, he had prevailed upon them to escort him to Wang-ba! Doubtless, if he would permit, they would take him into the presence of the man himself! Wentworth, changing into dry yachting clothing which he had found, smiled slightly at the conception. He would be spotted by lieutenants of Wang-ba long before he could achieve any such goal, of course. The most that he could hope for would be entrance into the place.

After that... The smile faded from his lips as he remembered his previous invasion of such an Oriental redoubt. There had been a hundred death traps and more than fifty police had perished in an attempt to follow where he led. There had been fungus whose spores had sprouted in human flesh, poisoned needles, pits of poisonous dust, dens of deadly vermin. And he had dared to think that victory was almost at hand! Good God, he had barely taken the first step toward the capture or death of Wang-ba!

Wentworth dropped upon one of the lockers and set to cleaning and oiling his guns. He could do nothing about the cartridges except set them where heat from the exhaust would strike them and hope that if they were wet, they soon would dry. He frowned, remembering how it had been necessary to shoot Malloy through the arm. The fool! He shrugged and, finishing his job on the guns, he went on deck to see where the boat was heading. The Chinese at the helm was keeping close to the New Jersey shore and the Statue of Liberty, on Bedloe's Island, was dropping rapidly behind. The bow was pointed toward Staten Island!

Of course! It was so logical a selection for headquarters that Wentworth wondered he had not guessed it. Wang-ba had operated on water from the first and, outside of New York and the Brooklyn shore of the East River, Staten Island offered the best refuge—and deeper water for the submarine. Wentworth was too elated at the nearness of his goal to feel the weariness that must have drugged his very soul. It was his third night, with only two hours sleep. His rugged frame was inured to hardship, but the secret wells of his strength had been sapped by so many, many battles. That must account for the heaviness that dragged now at his arms and limbs, that beat upon his brain in slow, numbing waves.

He went forward and sat upon the deck, leaned his shoulders against the cabin. He should make some plans for his behavior on reaching Wang-ba's stronghold. Impossible, of course, to do so definitely. It would depend on the situation of the place, on the behavior of the two men with him and on how soon his masquerade was discovered.

One thing he could do. He could leave a message in his clothing on the boat. Wang-ba would be certain to order the craft sent away and, when the stolen boat was found, the first thing police would do would be to examine the strange clothing found upon it. In that way, he might lead them to the place if he failed in his attempt tonight. Wentworth got paper and pencil, wrote rapidly, noted the bearings taken by the boat. It was very near the shore of Staten Island now and, suddenly, Wentworth knew where they were going. The Municipal Docks!

THE DOCKS had long been almost deserted. They had been built by Mayor Hylan in boom days and were known jeeringly as Hylan's Folly. They had cost millions—and they had scarcely been used. They made a perfect hiding place for Wang-ba. Deep water for his boats, acres of sheds to hide his supplies and his murder weapons, his scores of Chinese slaves… Wentworth saw that the motorboat turned in by the fourth wharf from the north and, jotting that down, made haste to put the paper in a pocket of his cape. He got his guns and reloaded them with bullets that almost burnt his fingers and slipped them into his holsters. There was a slight smile on the sinister face of the Spider. He was ready for the invasion!

Wentworth kept to the shadow of the cabin while the boat, engine cut, drifted head-on toward a bulk-head. The Chinese at the wheel uttered the low, wailing cry with which Wentworth had signaled them. It was not answered and the boat drifted on. It was barely ten feet from the bulkhead, now five... There was an abrupt roiling of the water against the concrete heading and, soundlessly, except for a spattering of drops, the bulkhead retreated before them and slid majestically to one side. Wentworth's lips were tight against his teeth. Small good that note to the police would do if he were captured! They would not find this means of entrance in a year of searching! Wang-ba had not been content to use the docks. He had made his headquarters *under them.*

As the boat drifted with its momentum through the opening in the wharf, Wentworth sent his eyes exploring the way ahead. He could see nothing in the impenetrable blackness, but to each side, he made out concrete pilings that formed an almost solid wall. There was a faint glimmer of light from without, but abruptly, even that was cut off by the closing of the secret door. There was a moment of intense, black waiting, then dim incandescents glowed overhead and Wentworth could see that the corridor through which the boat moved extended another fifty feet to a wharf. No one was in sight.

The momentum of the boat had died and the two Chinese with him were propelling it toward the wharf by pushing on the concrete piles with boat hooks. One of them ran forward to the extreme bow and leaned there, tensely, with the boat hook poised toward the ceiling. Just after he passed one of the dim, overhead bulbs, he stabbed up into the darkness. There was a rasping creak and a steel arm looped down and moved forward, as if it embraced something in the ceiling. When the boat passed under it, Wentworth saw what it was that it embraced, a port-cullis of three-foot spikes with needle points. If a boat passed under that, without first having touched that secret spring, it would be crushed to the bottom with a dead crew impaled on those spikes!

Wentworth's eyes held a hard, wary light. Well, he had expected things like this, hadn't he? And it was not only this passage that would be so guarded. Every lane, every hall of the headquarters that lay ahead would be protected by similar, and even more horrible, traps. Hopeless for him to attempt to tread them without a guide. He felt a tightening of all his muscles, a rippling along the back of his neck. He had entered the portals of death. God alone knew when, if ever, he would emerge!

CHAPTER 10
TRAPS OF TERROR

I T WAS Richard Wentworth's curse that he always saw very clearly how much depended on each maneuver of his many warfares. He thought, watching the boat warp slowly toward the dim-lit wharf, "If I fail tonight, Wang-ba will kill four thousand people tomorrow evening. The next night he will double that number and there will be no peace save in submission."

No conceit was implicit in his thought. He had been extraor-dinarily lucky to come this far without interference. There was small reason to think that any of the police would have the same fortune and, without it, discovery of this secret stronghold was almost impossible. It was strictly up to the Spider—one man against God alone knew how many scores of murderous Chinese—and he was on unfamiliar terrain that was full of pitfalls!

Yet, there was no faltering in his steady courage, no tremor over what might happen if he failed—for the Spider did not intend to fail! His whole body was relaxed and ready, every sense was attuned to its utmost, but without tension. When the need came for action, Wentworth would move with the smooth perfection of a grooved machine. There was one small spot of worry in his brain—that his guns might not operate in extremity. The cartridges were of uncertain value… His lips straightened a little grimly. He would do well not to resort to his automatics unless there was no other way out.

There was a light jar as the motorboat touched the concrete wharf. The bowman sprang ashore and carried a line with him. Wentworth waited until he had made fast, then stepped calmly to the wharf. His danger was not here in the dim light with his face shadowed under a peaked yachting cap. He looked about. A passage led from the wharf. He delayed, pretending to make sure that the boat was securely fastened, until one of the men with a show of reluctance entered the corridor that slanted off into darkness that was like the darkness of death….

Wentworth followed, keeping a casual, keen eye on his movements. He saw that, walking through the curve in the corridor that he could just make out, the man hugged the left-hand wall. Wentworth lengthened his stride, frowning. Within seconds, he would entirely lose sight of the man and, after that, how could he be sure of avoiding the traps he knew beset his path? He could not call for the other to wait and, since the Chinese did not, he could not use the pocket flashlight he had transferred from his wet clothing.

Even as he started forward, the man disappeared. Wentworth rounded the curve, pressing close to the wall as he had seen the other do, and stood still. There was not a sound from the passage ahead, not even the whisper of a felt slipper or the drip of water from the man's wet clothing. Wentworth felt the tension of his own waiting. He shrugged. There was only one thing to do, wait for the second man.

Wentworth squatted on his heels close against the wall and drew cigarettes from his pocket, tucked one between his lips. It would give him an excuse… asking for a light. He waited and slow seconds were prolonged into minutes. Wentworth began to feel the rhythm of his pulses. It communicated itself presently to the dim silence about him so that it, too, seemed to swell and recede with a faint roaring. Where in the devil was the second Chinese? Surely, he could have tied up a half-dozen boats by now? Wentworth's lips felt cold against his teeth. He rubbed a palm along his thigh, drew an automatic. There was no need to go to the wharf to look. What had happened was obvious. The first Chinese, returning unexpectedly, had given the alarm and Wang-ba had summoned the second man by some other secret passage. Soon now, very soon, he would come to inspect this man who had tricked his underlings into bringing him to the stronghold…!

WENTWORTH RESISTED an impulse to return to the wharf, there to wait and fight it out with the men who must presently come. His lips smiled slowly. If men were coming, they would already be here. This was a waiting game. He replaced his automatic, drew out a small platinum lighter and flicked flame to his cigarette, rested his head against the wall and smoked. Minutes dragged on and he did not move, save occasionally to light another cigarette....

It must have been more than an hour after he had taken his position there that a voice seemed to speak at his elbow. Wentworth did not turn his head, remembering that other occasion when words, without source, had sounded in his brain.

"Fools wait for death," said the voice. "A brave man goes to meet it."

The voice was the soft, slurring woman's contralto he had heard before. He laughed gently, but made no other reply and the silence once more ruled the darkness. Calmly, Wentworth lighted another cigarette. He was strangely confident, even exhilarated.

"Tell Wang-ba," he pronounced into the darkness, "that the Spider comes to talk with the Turtle."

His voice whispered off down the corridor, repeating with faint echoes, "with the Turtle... with the Turtle...." He smoked two more cigarettes, saw that there were only four more in his case of platinum and black enamel and closed it regretfully. Those cigarettes were all narcoticized. He waited, after that, in silence and darkness.

Presently, he became aware that there was a faint lessening of the blackness about him. He was not at first sure of the source of the light, if, indeed, it could be called light, but his eyes drooped over his lids and a slight smile touched his lips. Wang-ba had grown impatient of waiting and wished to bring matters to a crisis. Well, the Spider was ready.

The darkness took on a greenish tinge, not actual light, but a green blackness that seemed tangible. Wentworth realized that he could see his hands, shining up at him as if they were coated with radium. A curse pushed against his locked teeth. A radium exposure could kill a man, but it would take a considerable while. He sat unmoving and wished for another cigarette, guessing that Wang-ba sought to break his composure.

By degrees as indistinguishable as the movements of clock hands, the light increased until the entire hall shone with a green glow that seemed rather in the air than from any definite point. There was a faint draft through the corridor and it seemed to Wentworth that the green light whirled and danced before it like motes in a sunbeam. He became aware first of a conflicting movement; then of a figure that materialized out of the far dimness of the passageway, a slim girl in the trousers and long, embroidered jacket of the East. Her dress shimmered like the green sea, and her face....

"This light makes your lips ugly as hell," Wentworth told her, and he watched her mouth move in the cruel smile that once before had nearly heralded his death, when this same woman had held a death-adder's fangs close to his hand.

"The Turtle," she said in her fine deep voice, "bids welcome to the Spider and bids him into the Presence."

Wentworth rose lithely, without stiffness, to his feet. He

bowed with the formal elegance his friends knew so well, despite the awkward hunch he put into his shoulders.

"After you, Almond Flower," he said.

SHE TURNED and Wentworth took two long strides and was beside her, a hand circling her arm just above the elbow, closing tightly, not on soft flesh, but on muscles that slid as smoothly as snakes beneath the skin.

"If there are trap-doors beneath the floor," he said, smiling, "we shall go through them together."

The woman's long eyes slid toward him and her lips continued their smile. Wentworth thought that there was a touch of malicious pleasure in their expression. His left hand crossed his chest and slid out an automatic, which he nuzzled against her side.

"I once saw a man shot through the side with a forty-five caliber bullet," he said conversationally. "It made just the tiniest hole where it went in, but it blew his entire viscera out the other side. I doubt if anything that happened to me would be quick enough to keep my finger from pulling the trigger."

There was a change in the smile on the woman's face. Her pale lips, purple under the green light, writhed like bruised snakes. She advanced ten paces down the hall and stood for a dozen heartbeats stationary, then she moved on, and Wentworth surmised some death-trap had been evaded thereby. Her eyes slid time and again to Wentworth's face and there was murder in their glint, but there was respect, too. Presently her right hand pressed a seam of concrete as they went past and a little while later she paused to wave her hand first on one side and then the other of a dark electric globe in the ceiling. Wentworth felt chilled, wondering what ghastly deaths he would have met had he threaded through these passages alone. The woman turned toward him with her eyes half-closed.

"If I had waved my hand on just one side," she informed him pleasantly, "an ounce of Devil Flame would have dropped upon your skull. It would not have killed you instantly, but the pain would have made it impossible for you to hurt me."

Wentworth smiled directly into her eyes. "Thank you. You are very generous." His own eyes were mocking.

They reached a point where stairs led upward and where there seemed no other means of passage. She put one foot on the first step and stamped twice. The wall on her right receded slowly, noiselessly and then slipped aside. She led the way through the opening and gestured toward a spot below the stairs they had not climbed. Wentworth felt his teeth rasp together, knew that his hand tightened on the woman's arm.

There was a pit beneath the steps and it swam with green light. The place was alive with tiny crawling things that were shut in by glass walls, ants, thousands, millions of ants. They crawled over the gleaming white bones of a human being, to whose skull fragments of long blond hair still clung.

"In heaven's name," Wentworth whispered, "who was that?"

The woman's laughter was snarling. "A woman of whom the Master tired," she said, caressingly. "The ants must sometimes be fed."

Wentworth felt nausea squirming like a snake in his belly, but he forced himself to dissemble. He laughed. "Can't we go a

little faster?" he asked gently. "I am anxious to meet this delight-
ful chap."

The woman looked at him curiously. "I think that you are
quite brave," she said. "The Master will be glad that you evaded
his traps."

"Yes?"

"Yes, he can devise much slower and more pleasant ways of
testing your courage!"

"You interest me," Wentworth told her dryly.

THEY HAD passed no doors that he could distinguish in
the solid walls. The corridor had turned and twisted until he
was hard put to remember directions, but he believed that they
had gone to the shore, and were now approaching the third pier.
Despite his determination, his invincible courage, Wentworth
knew a feeling of utter futility. Amid this labyrinth, what chance
had a lone man? Even if he destroyed Wang-ba, would not this
woman and the other members of his organization carry on?
How could he hope to triumph over the legion of his enemies?

The woman said, "I have to use both hands here."

"Do you have to use your throat, too?" Wentworth asked
gently.

The woman's lips writhed and she cursed him in burning,
monosyllabic Chinese. She had, Wentworth discerned, a nice
gift for idiom.

"You still haven't answered my question," he reminded her.
There was a grim coldness in his voice that choked off her words.
She bowed her head toward him.

"By all means, strangle me," she said flatly.

Wentworth released his hold on her arm, flicked his hand with lightning speed toward her throat. But swift as he was, she was faster. Or rather, she had less to do. She only threw her weight upon her right foot, which rested on a ridge between two areas of cement upon the floor. Wentworth felt the earth move beneath him. A despairing cry rose in his throat. He snatched at the woman, caught the hem of her blouse. His gun hand caught on the firm section of the floor where she stood. She was leaning back against his pull, but suddenly, with tightening lips, she threw her entire weight upon his head. Together, they spun off into darkness.

Wentworth had a glimpse of the floor closing above him. Then, in utter blackness, he struck a padded bottom. He was instantly on his feet. The air here smelled very clean, rich in ozone. He felt its mad exhilaration in his blood, in the pounding of his heart. He still had the hem of the woman's blouse, but when he tried to reach her, he found only the silken garment, limp in his hand. About him was no sound at all—no hint of pain or death—but he realized with an abysmal, sudden terror, that his head was spinning, that his senses were reeling in a drunken frenzy.

He groped for his cigarette lighter, struck it to flame and the fire leaped high and higher until it seemed to fill the tiny chamber in which Wentworth found himself. He could stretch out his arms and touch all four walls. It was empty except for himself. He looked dazedly at the silken garment in his hand. Then the flame winked out, and darkness in which there were tiny darting points of red began to swim before his eyes.

Wentworth sank upon his knees, a wry smile on his lips. So, the Spider would invade the Turtle's stronghold and kill him, would he? He laughed, wildly, crazily, gulped… and pitched forward on his face. The red points vanished. He sank into imponderable darkness….

CHAPTER 11
THE MERCY OF WANG-BA

WENTWORTH RETURNED to consciousness with an abruptness that startled his heart. There was no pain, no headache. He opened his eyes in full possession of his senses—and looked into the flaming black orbs of Wang-ba.

"How do you like my new anesthetic, Wentworth *san?*" the yellow monster asked solicitously. "I have not tried it personally, but I understand from others that it is quite the most nearly perfect thing of its kind. A little experiment of mine with ozone and… shall we say, kindred gases?"

Wentworth bowed, his face expressionless. "Of all the ways in which I have taken leave of my senses," he said, casually, "your gas is the gentlest."

He glanced about and found that Wang-ba and he were alone in a vast chamber whose walls were silken drapes of the same peculiar shade of green that had taken the form of light in the dark corridor. Hope sprang full-fledged into his heart, but he held it down cautiously. He knew, by his arms against his sides, that he was without his weapons. And from Wang-ba's manner of address, he realized that his Spider disguise had been stripped

"There are other rewards
less merciful!"

from his face. Still, if he were quick of movement, he might kill Wang-ba by certain nerve pressures in the throat before help could reach him.

His eyes turned back to the face of Wang-ba and the Chinese was smiling. Wentworth knew with a sudden certainty that the man had read his thought and that he had made provisions against such an attempt. Wentworth shrugged his shoulders slightly, waited for Wang-ba to speak. There was no denying the desperate character of his situation. He had been captured in what was obviously an attempt to reach and kill this man, but he would not give up hope. He would yet discover some means to accomplish his ends... Wentworth moved his legs—he was seated with them folded beneath him—and discovered that they were linked together, apparently by some sort of ankle-cuff. It was just as well that he had no attempted to spring upon Wang-ba before....

The single note of a gong hummed through the air of the room and Wentworth heard the rustle of silken drapes. Wang-ba's voice purred like a cars.

"The two men who brought you here are due for a slight reprimand," he said softly. "In the first place, they fled from my enemies before I came to release them. In the second place, their dereliction permitted more than twenty food trains to get through to New York—"

Wentworth smiled with pleasure at the news. Malloy, then, had not permitted the arm wound to prevent him from carrying on. A brave and competent man, if one could overlook the battle-madness that had almost destroyed Wentworth's carefully laid plans. Not that his carrying out of those plans had accomplished much. Wang-ba's voice droned on....

"... and they allowed themselves to be tricked by an enemy—yourself, Wentworth *san*—into bringing that enemy to my doors. These were tactical errors...."

A shivering moan pulled Wentworth's head about and he saw the two Chinese who had come with him crouched upon their knees, foreheads pressed to the floor.

"Mercy, Master!" one pleaded. "This one said that he came in thy great name and he gave the signal cry. We could not know...."

"Yes, yes," purred Wang-ba and a coldness crept over Wentworth's limbs at the tone of his voice. "Because I realize the cleverness of him who fooled you, your punishment shall be merciful." He paused, but neither of the men lifted his head, nor did their shivering cease. "You shall only die the death of Wang-ba!"

A quavering shriek was drawn from the two men, but the four powerful guards who stood behind them yanked them to their feet and dragged them away. The light in the room began to fade and, with a faint silken rustling, the curtains were drawn away from a section of the wall opposite Wang-ba. As the illumination continued to fade in the room and to brighten at the same time where the curtains had lifted, Wentworth saw that there was a glass-sided tank of water and in it swam—*turtles!* With a curse of amazement, Wentworth studied the huge reptiles. He recognized them instantly, the huge wolf-turtles, of whose flesh the Chinese were inordinately fond. They had savage parrot-beaks. Even as the significance of the tank made a sick paralysis grip all his body, Wentworth saw a heavy anchor, with a rope about it, sink slowly down into the pool. The rope showed for eighteen inches and then, a man's feet, bound to the anchor.

Wentworth's breath burned his throat. "You foul fiend!" he whispered. "You promised those men mercy!"

Wang-ba laughed and Wentworth knew that his face remained impassive. "Did not my Little White Flower show you the pit of the ants? That is one of my slightly less merciful methods. And there are—*others!*"

A THIN, wavering scream of ultimate agony came faintly into the room where Wentworth sat, his feet chained immovably to the floor. A deadly fascination swung his eyes toward the turtle tank. One of the great reptiles was swimming toward the beach which was just visible at one end and there was something in its mouth from which thin, dark waving lines of liquid floated away. Above the anchor, the water was darkening and there were other turtles moving toward the spot, their beaks snapping inaudibly....

Wentworth's jaw set with the rigidness of iron and waves of burning rage swept up to engulf his brain. The wailing continued, beating upon his ears like a tocsin. But he knew he was helpless. His hands had gone to the shackles on his ankles and he found that not only were the chains fastened to the floor, but his crossed ankles were fastened to the opposite leg so that he could only sit there and listen, listen....

He turned his furious eyes to the face of Wang-ba. The man was incredible—a mad beast to be slain without mercy.

"For God's sake," Wentworth whispered. "Kill the man."

Wang-ba lifted one shoulder slightly, his eyes unwavering on the tank. "He is immersed almost to the waist. Before I could summon anyone here, he would be dead. Really, it is a quite merciful death, this of the turtles, and after all, *my pets must be fed!*"

Wentworth lunged toward Wang-ba, but the Chinese did not even flinch away. He turned his impassive face toward the Spider, who had only succeeded in badly wrenching his legs.

"You have just demonstrated, Wentworth *san*," Wang-ba purred, "the weakness of the West—the thing that will make it simple for us of the East to rule over you. You do not know these men. In fact, they would have slain you long ago had they known your identity. Yet, you can not bear to see them suffer. No, no, Wentworth *san*, I am prepared to respect your intellect and your courage, but your wisdom—*tch, tch!*" The clucking noise he made with his tongue somehow calmed Wentworth. He knew that the second Chinese was now being lowered into the vat of torture, for the quality of the screams differed a little. He was racked with hatred, with loathing for this creature beside him, but a display of temper would not win release and victory over the beast.

Wentworth forced himself to laugh. "Some day, Wang-ba," he predicted cheerfully, "the brother of one of these men you torture or the women you destroy is going to slice your throat neatly from ear to ear."

Wang-ba chuckled. "It will be a pity. You had rather fancied that pleasant task for yourself, had you not? Ah, look Wentworth, *san*, the strength of the human body under pain is rather remarkable, is it not? Our second man has succeeded in lifting the anchor. I am delighted. He has earned further mercy." He struck the gong beside him and the screams ceased. Wentworth dared to turn his eyes toward the tank and saw a headless trunk sinking slowly amid the worrying turtles. While he looked, the head, too, was tossed into the water and the curtains dropped over the blood-soiled scene.

Wentworth felt as if he were strangling. The air was too close, too thick, to breathe. He threw back his head and sucked in great lungfuls and gradually faintness left him. When he looked up, he was alone. He well understood the strategy of Wang-ba. The Chinese had left him with that picture of incredible horror before him—the curtain had been drawn from before the tank again—and knew that inevitably the question must arise in Wentworth's brain: What will my own fate be? Certainly, nothing so "merciful" as the turtle tank.

Resolutely, Wentworth drove his horror-sick brain away from the scenes he had witnessed. He had only himself to lean upon, and a city's life depended on him. Somehow, and quickly, he must contrive release from these fetters and strike at Wang-ba. It was not a question of possibilities. It was a matter of necessity. Wentworth's lips twisted wryly.

"I am not yet dead," he whispered. That thought was his only hope....

WENTWORTH EXAMINED the chains upon his legs. They were light, but all his straining could not so much as bend one link. There were no locks. While he had been unconscious, the metal bands had been welded together. Something very much like despair crept up in Wentworth's breast. He recognized the cruelty of the Chinese in the lightness of the chains. If he were a little stronger, he might snap them, but there was no way to gain a purchase on the fetters. It was mental torture of the shrewdest kind.

The thought of torture lifted Wentworth's eyes again to the glass tank in which the turtles swam. He saw the beak of one that weighed close to two hundred pounds close upon the stripped thigh bone of one of the two tortured men. It snapped in two like a dry stick. Wentworth's breath caught in his throat. He looked swiftly about him. The gong upon which Wang-ba had struck swung from a golden arch by little golden chains and the whole thing rested upon a small teakwood table. Was it heavy enough?

Wentworth dug his fingers into the silken carpet on which he and Wang-ba had sat and dragged it toward him. The table with the gong wobbled slightly, but moved. The gong swayed on its golden chains and a faint silvery note came from it. Wentworth's lips set solidly. He glanced toward the silk-draped walls, but there was no indication there that he was watched. If only the gong-stand was heavy enough…!

At last, his eager hands closed on the table and he drew the gong toward him. He lifted the thing and there was a pleasure in the touch. It was heavy enough to be solid gold! With a wrench, he snapped the gong from its golden chains—if only his own fetters would break so easily!—and looked at the turtle tank with coldly calculating eyes. He would have only one try. That one must be enough… He weighed the gong stand in his hand, then drew it over his head with both arms, leaned far back. He poised like that while he gathered the electric energy of his body into his muscles. Then, with a sharp exhalation, he swept body and arms forward and hurled the golden stand with all his strength squarely at the glass side of the turtle tank!

If Wentworth knew the fearful risk he took, his face gave no indication. His eyes blazed with hope, and there was an eager quirk to his lips. He choked back a shout of joy when the gold stand, far from bouncing back futilely as he half-feared it might, smashed entirely through the glass side of the tank near its base! Star-like cracks radiated in all directions from the break and as the water gushed out through the opening, spurting half across the room, those cracks widened, spread and, suddenly, the entire side of the tank collapsed and spewed over the floor hundreds of gallons of water, what was left of the two bodies—and twelve huge turtles…!

The pressure had been greater than Wentworth had estimated and the rush of water swept over him, hurled him backward as it poured across the room. It was done in an instant and he heard frightened cries resounding through the apartments adjoining the chamber where he sat helpless upon the floor.

Wentworth hurriedly sat erect. He still clung to the small teak-wood table and the gong and he threw a quick glance about the room, seeking out the fierce wolf-turtles. Three lay on their backs, impotently moving their flippers in an attempt to right themselves, which they could not do. One apparently had been washed through a hidden door in the wall, for he had disappeared. The other eight were oaring themselves awkwardly about on the floor. Their cruel beaks were open as if they hissed, but no sound came through their jaws.

Wentworth watched them warily, his grim face a little white under its tan. He had seen what those beaks could do. He knew that he would be hard put to fight off even one of the monsters when they moved to attack him as, inevitably, they would. But that was a risk he was prepared to take. If he remained a prisoner of Wang-ba, some even more horrible death was designed for him. Better to take the chance of freedom—and death…!

FIVE OF the eight turtles still able to move about presently resumed their horrible feasting, but the other three moved about with seeming aimlessness, awkwardly barging their weight on inadequate flippers. Wentworth found that his breath was quickening in his throat. The shrill cries of the Chinese wavered back and forth in the hallways and one yellow, frightened face thrust through the curtains, to be immediately drawn back. The man's voice rose in frantic imprecations. "The turtle-tank!" he cried. "The turtle-tank is broken. They devour the prisoner!"

Not yet, Wentworth thought grimly, but one of them, a massive reptile with a barnacle-encrusted back, had centered his unwinking stare upon him. Now, with ponderous deliberation the fierce beast was shuffling toward him on rubbery flippers. Wolf turtles, they were called, and they were even more deadly in their attack. One grip with those razor-edged beaks… Well, he had played for just this, hadn't he? Deliberately smashed the tank so that one of the creatures would attack him and he could use it to win his way to freedom? But now that the trial he had foreseen was at hand, Wentworth felt a momentary doubt of his own abilities. After all, he was chained to the floor, unable to move. And the turtle would weigh nearly two hundred pounds.

Wentworth teetered up on his fettered knees, the teak table in one hand, gong in the other. Feeble weapons with which to overcome that monster! And now the thing which Wentworth had dreaded above all others was occurring. Another of the turtles was waddling to the attack and—Good God!—both of them would reach him at almost the same instant! Surely this was the strangest battle that ever any man had fought since those ancient days when giant lizards roamed the earth. A curved piece of metal and a tiny table for weapons against creatures which could snap a man's thigh in two with their powerful jaws!

Yet Wentworth smiled as the two turtles moved on him. One was lagging a little behind the other. It only required perfect timing, perfect nerves.

"Come on, Wolfie!" he shouted. "I'm betting on old barnacle-back!"

A Chinese who peered in at that instant cried out that the white man had gone mad; that he was coaxing the turtles to kill him. Where was Wang-ba, Wentworth wondered, that he did not come to interfere with this perilous game he played? Surely, it was not already night, nor had Wang-ba gone to claim his third toll of human lives in New York? Wentworth discovered that he had no conception at all of the time, due to his period of unconsciousness, which might have lasted one hour or a dozen.

These thoughts flitted through Wentworth's brain as his eyes flicked from one to the other of the two wolves flippering toward

148

him. They were no more than six feet away, approaching at diagonals that would bring them to his right and left almost simultaneously. He had only one salvation, their slowness of movement, and that did not apply to the lightning darts of their huge, beaked heads. They would be as swift-moving as a snake....

Four feet, now three away. In another instant, one of them would be close enough for the maneuver Wentworth planned. One of them, only a scant two feet away, paused and twisted its vicious head to one side to stare at this strange prey kneeling, waiting for its attack. In that instant, Wentworth took his chance. The other turtle had its beak open, straining forward to strike. With a quick movement, Wentworth thrust the teakwood table at its face. There was a rending of strong wood as the beak closed hard upon the object.

Wentworth sliced down at the back of the creature's head with the edge of the gong, then seized a flipper and dragged the reptile sideways toward him. It was ticklish, deadly work. The turtle could reach its front flipper with its head, if it dropped the teakwood table. Only its stupidity in clinging to the bait Wentworth had offered saved him. Now Wentworth had hold of the back flipper and his hands were out of danger. But the second turtle was moving in now. It had to circle to get around its companion whom Wentworth had tricked and Wentworth for the moment had no defense save that.

FRANTICALLY, HE gripped the flipper and the side of the barnacle-encrusted shell with both hands. He hunched his shoulders, put all his strength into a single upward heave. There would be time for no more. Already the second turtle was within eighteen inches of his arm. The first turtle went up on its side with Wentworth's heave, wavered, then at a new and savage thrust, toppled over on its back.

Wentworth flung himself away from the savage beak of the second monster with only scant inches to spare. He caught up the gong and offered it as bait for the gaping jaws. With a snap, the turtle struck. The fine metal rang under the bite of the beak. The razor-edges sliced through the curve of its rim, began to cut toward its center. There was not an instant to lose. Wentworth seized a flipper, heaved to spin that cruel head away. He heaved again. His chest labored; sweat stood out on his face, made a thin coating on his arms and throat. His heart pounded against his ribs. Then the turtle was on its side and flopped over on its back.

Wentworth reeled back from his labors, threw a swift glance about the room. A Chinese, stepping warily, was trying to turn one of the wolves over on its back, but he had nothing to offer its jaws and the head struck and struck again, kept him dancing. He dodged from the room, shouting for help.

There was no time for Wentworth to rest. At any moment, the Chinese might return in force and all his efforts would be in vain. Wentworth seized one of the overturned turtles and maneuvered it so that the head would be toward him. Its flippers moved aimlessly, unable to touch the floor. The head was hampered in half its movements, and the turtle could see almost nothing.

If what Wentworth had done before was dangerous, what he proposed now was suicidal. He must maneuver the chain that bound his ankle to his opposite knee into the beak of the turtle. Once that was accomplished, he had small doubt of the outcome, but to get just that short bit of chain into the jaws, yet protect his flesh....

Wentworth reared on his knees, waited his chance and seized the rubbery neck of the turtle from below with both hands. The reptile writhed and twisted, using that grip as a point of leverage to move its whole body. All Wentworth's weight, all his strength was pressing down upon that neck and despite his best efforts, the head moved. He would have to chance it like that. Slowly, with infinite caution, he wriggled the lower part of his body toward the beak. His only salvation now was that the turtle could scarcely see anything and Wentworth, grinding its head against the floor, hampered it even more. He got the chain into the turtle's beak and the gaping jaws snapped venomously shut.

Instantly, Wentworth flung himself backward, putting all his weight against the chain. The razor beak—and Wentworth's wrench against its edges—accomplished what his lone strength had failed to do. The chain snapped. Now he had that same task to perform over again, to free the other ankle. It was split-second work, but he achieved it, and freed of his chains, he cast a harried look about him. He had only got loose in time. Through a door on the far side of the room came five Chinese with long bars of wood. They proceeded systematically to turn the turtles over on their backs.

Wentworth sat upon his legs, hiding the fact that the chains were broken beneath his body. He was panting from his exertions. The turtles he had succeeded in thrusting a little away from him so that he was no longer menaced by their beaks—in one of

151

which a fragment of chain was still held. If one of the Chinese saw that... Wentworth threw a hunted look about the room. The silk had been thoroughly wetted by the flood from the tank and he could see four doorways. There was no way of telling what lay beyond anyone of them. Undoubtedly, there would be traps, but these would be chiefly along the corridors that led to exits. The Chinese were paying him no attention, chattering among themselves in frightened tones.

"The Master will be like a wolf-turtle himself when he learns what happened."

"My be far away when he come back."

"Suppose we tell him prisoner break?"

Wentworth smiled thinly. There would probably be more of Wang-ba's "mercy" when he returned. These Chinese had given him both good and bad news. If Wang-ba was away, it would be easier for him to escape, but it meant also that he could not complete his task... Cautiously, Wentworth got to his feet. The Chinese still went about their task. One of the turtles had got its back to the wall and was snapping furiously at the men... Wentworth moved backward toward the door just behind him. He made the shadows without having been seen, turned—and looked into the leveled barrel of an automatic, held by the woman whom Wang-ba called his Little White Flower.

"You are very clever, Wentworth *san*," she murmured softly, "but I think I would prefer that you be here when Wang-ba returns!"

CHAPTER 12
THE FIRE GUNS

WENTWORTH WENT back on his heels. His breath blew out slowly and he was hard put to keep from hurling himself futilely against the muzzle of the woman's automatic. He knew it would be death, but, Good God, he had labored so hard to be free that he might fight for the salvation of the city! And now, the little accident of this woman and her gun....

Down the corridor where the woman held him, came the swift patter of felt slippers. A man's voice was crying thinly.

"The police!" he shouted. "The police come! Five boatloads come! Already their axes bite into the ceiling!"

Wentworth threw back his head and laughed. "You are doomed, White Flower, you and Wang-ba. My message has brought them!"

"Your message?" the woman's voice was strangely soft. "You had no chance to send a message."

Wentworth smiled into her impassive face. "Wang-ba sent the stolen boat away, didn't he?"

The woman nodded and Wentworth shrugged. "I had written a message and secreted it on the boat, that is all."

The woman's eyes, oddly, shone with admiration. "And when you broke the turtle tank, the water, leaking out, betrayed which dock we were using."

Dimly, through the corridors, came the battering sound of axes. The woman was very calm. She lifted her voice. "Bring guns of the Devil Flame!" she cried. She turned to Wentworth. "It is a shame that a man so brave, so intelligent, should waste his time in honesty. You are almost as great as Wang-ba."

Wentworth shrugged. "I am stronger than Wang-ba," he said. "If you'll take me to him, I will prove it." He had small hope that he could persuade the woman, but there was a chance....

"He overcame you with his will," the woman was sneering. "He made you almost kill your best friend!"

Wentworth's hand lifted and touched the tiny wound that still marked his cheek. "He did not overcome me with his will," he said shortly. "His will was failing before mine and he had me shot, here. Afterward, he killed the man who fired the dart with my own gun, lest it be known that I had beaten his will."

The woman stared at him with dark equivocal eyes for a long moment, then she shook her head. "I do not believe you," she replied curtly. Wentworth shrugged again. She shouted a new order in Chinese and men ran past them in the corridor with the crossbows and quivers of glass-tipped bolts. But Wentworth had no chance to snatch at the automatic in her hand. She held him competently, without trembling. Her hand was braced against her hip, lest it tire. Wentworth's eyes narrowed as he watched her. He could see a bright patch on the barrel of the automatic. There was a small rust fleck on the trigger guard. Suddenly he knew. That was his gun! Undoubtedly, it still held the cartridges that had been wetted in his long swim across the river. Would they fire?

Wentworth put his eyes on hers. "My will is stronger than the will of Wang-ba," he said flatly. "My will is stronger than yours!"

The woman's eyes widened a little under his stare. The smile stiffened on her lips and Wentworth could see her bracing herself for a battle of wills. She straightened a little and in that instant, Wentworth sprang. His left hand caught the gun barrel and twisted it aside. He laughed as the bullet blasted past within an inch of his side. Strange! The thing that had actuated him in his attempt was a hope that the gun might not fire. It had discharged, but he was master of the situation anyway.

With a wrench, he had the gun. His right hand had gone into the woman's face and driven her back hard against the wall of the corridor so that she collapsed onto the floor, unconscious. For half a second, Wentworth stood looking down on her. She had courage, this Little White Flower of Wang-ba.

The Chinese would wreak his vengeance and his rage over this raid on her... Wentworth shook his head. That was not his concern. She should have chosen her companions with a better eye toward her own safety....

HE WHIRLED to glance up and down the corridor, saw a Chinese with a cross-bow leveled at his back Wentworth flung aside and squeezed the trigger. The hammer clicked emptily, but he had dodged the bolt. Down the hall sped the fire-bolt and there was a flash of greenish flame far away in the darkness. Wentworth flung the automatic violently at the Chinese and caught him in the forehead. The man went backward without a sound.

Wentworth whirled and stared back where the fire bolt had spread. Green flame was dripping from the ceiling and, spreading with hellish rapidity, was sweeping along the hall. Once more Wentworth stared down at the inert body of the Little White Flower. With a curse, he caught her up and threw her over his shoulder. If he could leave her to face the wrath of Wang-ba, he could not leave her to be burned alive by the Devil Flame. Wentworth paused to catch up the crossbow and quiver of fire bolts from beside the Chinese he had felled. He hesitated a moment, then he stooped again over the body from which he had hammered all life and touched the base of his cigarette lighter to the forehead. When he straightened and strode rapidly away, carrying the light body of White Flower, a crimson spot glistened on the forehead of the dead man, a spot that had hairy, crooked legs and poised fangs, *the seal of the Spider!*

If police penetrated here, Wang-ba would learn from the newspapers that his enemy lived, that the Spider had struck this blow at the monster who threatened the Western world!

But Wentworth could not immediately beat a retreat, even if he had known the direction into which to flee. He followed the corridor down which he had seen men run with the flame guns. That, evidently, was where White Flower had set the line of defense. There, the Spider would have to go if he was to open this hell-dive to the police.

A corner of the corridor showed a wide room whose far wall was concrete. Through loopholes, the Chinese were firing with their cross-bows, pausing between shots to wind back the bow-string with the double crank at the end of the stock. Wentworth put White Flower gently down upon the floor and cranked back his own bow. His face was set with grim purpose. He was without his usual weapons. He would have to turn those of the men of Wang-ba back upon them. When the cross-bow was drawn to its full-length, he peered again into the room of loopholes. Against the far wall, he saw a case of the Devil Flame bolts.

There was something implacable about the face of the Spider as he lifted the cross-bow to his shoulder. He might have been an embodiment of all the stern judges of mankind. He was destiny and retribution; he was the defender of the white races. He laid the cross-bow on the bin of fire bolts and released the cord from the trigger stem.

The fire-bolt hissed forward. Wentworth did not even wait to see the results of his shot. He did not need to. He snatched up the woman's body and fled, light-footed, along the corridor. Behind him, there came a gust of air, then an unholy burst of greenish flame. For a space of seconds, human voices raised in terror and pain echoed through the concrete hall—and then all was silence save for the booming roar of the spreading fire.

Wentworth fled through the room of the turtles, dodging the three which still remained right side up, and went out the door on the opposite side. Then he paused, looked desperately about. There were corridors, but they were full of traps of unholy death. For a moment, he thought of trying to revive the woman he carried, but he knew with a grim certainty that she would defy him, choose to perish here in this fire trap rather than lead him to safety. Why, then, should he bother about her?

The hard, thin lips of the Spider smiled a little. This was the weakness of the Western races, Wang-ba had said, that they believed in and practiced humanity. Well... Wentworth placed

White Flower once more upon the floor and took up the cross-bow. There were two ways of escape, up and down. The fire-bolts could open both passages.

Cranking back the string of the bow, Wentworth sent two swift shots, one against the ceiling fifty feet down the hall, one against the floor. The flame splashed away from him and he watched grimly to see the result. The green flame upon the ceiling flickered out after a while, but that on the floor licked higher and higher and ate its way furiously through wood panels....

Leaving the woman behind him, Wentworth crept close to the hole and peered down. Not five feet below was the black glint of water. With a lighthearted laugh, Wentworth returned to White Flower, caught her up in his arms. He checked clear of the burning edge of the hole in the floor, then sprang wide and shot down into the cold depths of the water below the flaming stronghold of Wang-ba....

WENTWORTH COULD do little to check his descent into the black water. He held the woman with one arm and with the other hand prevented her from breathing water into her lungs. The chill struck through to his bones in one agonizing second.

Long before he had begun to kick his way toward the surface again, the woman was stirring feebly in his arms. Wentworth told himself that it was madness—this thing he did in saving the woman who was evidently Wang-ba's chief agent—but it was useless even to think about it. He had chosen to rescue her.

His lungs were bursting when his head finally broke the surface. He looped an elbow beneath White Flower's chin and stroked strongly toward the edge of the pier. His arms and legs already felt numb under the frigid bite of the water. To his right, he could see the green glare of the Devil Flame where it had eaten through the flooring of Wang-ba's den. There were thin screamings that told of trapped men.

White Flower lay passive while he towed her toward open water. He was sure that she had recovered consciousness with the shock of the cold water, but she gave no sign of it. What would he do with her, Wentworth wondered. Turn her over to the police? He shrugged mentally. That probably was the better course. He would not be able to persuade her to betray Wang-ba, of that he was certain.

"Why did you save me?" the woman asked abruptly. "You set Wang-ba's hold on fire, then carried me out."

Wentworth was panting from the cold and from his strenuous efforts, weighted down as he was with his clothes, and, he suddenly remembered, the quiver of fire arrows he had slung over his shoulder.

"Couldn't leave you… to burn," he gasped out. "What Wang-ba would call… weakness of the West."

He was a little angry with himself. He had needlessly burdened himself with the woman. He had made new trouble, for if she escaped, she would carry the word of the holocaust to Wang-ba, arm him anew against his enemies.

"I can swim," said White Flower. Without waiting for him to release her, she abruptly twisted free of his arm and, when he whirled toward her—damn the woman; he would not let her escape!—she was swimming calmly beside him. Her teeth were chattering with the cold, but she continued to gasp questions at him.

"Back there in the hall... just a trick?" she asked. "A trick to throw me off guard... your story about Wang-ba?"

"Truth," Wentworth told her succinctly. "Man drugged me with dart... Wang-ba killed him. If Wang-ba's will was stronger... why did he drug me?"

White Flower swam in silence through a long moment. They were close to the edge of the pier now and out in the black water, dancing with the reflection of flames that leaped higher and higher into the night, five police-boats cruised slowly back and forth. Now and then, a man fired into the ruins of the dock or a fire-arrow burst on the water.

Wentworth put a cupped hand to his mouth. "Ahoy, police!" he shouted. "Wentworth with prisoner coming out. Don't shoot!"

"Prisoner!" gasped the woman beside him. There was a small flurry in the water and when he turned about, White Flower had vanished beneath the surface. He dived after her, failed to find any trace of the woman. He came back to the surface, gasping.

"Wentworth!" he heard a hail, recognizing it joyfully as the voice of Commissioner Flynn. "Wentworth, where are you?"

"Here!" he shouted. "Wait a minute. Prisoner escaped."

LIGHT, MOCKING laughter came to him somewhere from the darkness among the piles. "I could have killed you, Wentworth *san*," White Flower called, "with my knife; but I spared you, as you spared me. I would have been your faithful slave, Wentworth *san*, but I will not be a prisoner of the police."

Wentworth swam with his powerful racing stroke toward the

sound of the voice, but he could not find the woman. Finally, wearily, numbed with cold, he called again to the police and swam toward the boat that came to meet him. He was hauled out of the water and hurried into the cabin where Flynn helped him strip and dry himself, climb into some police clothes that were in the lockers.

"Got your note on the motorboat," Flynn said, his voice harsh, quick. "Couldn't find anything on fourth pier. Heard water leaking over here. Nice piece of work, Wentworth. Where is Wang-ba?"

Wentworth grinned up at the lean, tall Police Commissioner. Flynn's long, square head was covered with white bristly hair. His jaw was hard, muscle-knotted; his back was as stiff as a ramrod. He was a retired major-general of the regular army, and he ran his men with an iron hand that they had come to love.

"Wang-ba," Wentworth told him, "is probably preparing to kill his four thousand people in New York City, but we've got him, Flynn. By God, we've got him! We not only destroyed his main stronghold, but killed off most of his underlings. He'll only have the men who are with him."

Commissioner Flynn's face lengthened, his frosty blue eyes snapped. "Got him, hell," he burst out. "Kirkpatrick was kidnaped tonight!"

Wentworth jerked to his feet. "They got Kirk?" he cried.

Flynn stared at him without speaking.

Wentworth caught his shoulders. "Tell me about it," he said rapidly. "Has anything else happened?"

"Miss van Sloan," Flynn said shortly. "Lieutenant Governor. Four senators. Two of my deputies. Vice Mayor. All kidnaped."

Wentworth staggered back a step. "Ten people," he muttered. "Ten! Good God. *Nita...* Flynn, go on with it."

Flynn's hands were locked hard behind him. The shoulders bulged. "Their heads at noon tomorrow," he said, "unless the ransom is paid."

Wentworth stood staring into Flynn's face with incredulous eyes. Tomorrow at noon, if the ransom of a hundred million dollars was not paid, the heads of ten people would be delivered at military headquarters, the head of... of Governor Kirkpatrick, and... and of Nita! Good God in heaven, Nita's sweet, proud little head! A curse tore from his throat. He whirled on his heel, strode the length of the cabin and back again in a frenzied need for movement, for anything to break the horror of this moment.

"He can't, Flynn," he swore hoarsely. "He can't...."

He stopped, pulled himself together with a slow exertion of will. "Your men can finish this off, Flynn," he said woodenly. "Let's get back to New York. At any time, Wang-ba may strike. When he does, we must meet him and force some one of his men to tell where he has taken his prisoners. I'll get the truth out of him if I have to...."

He broke off. Flynn was looking into his face with haggard eyes, but there was a grim, hard set to his lips.

"By God," he rasped. "I'll help you with the torture!"

HE SWUNG about, his harsh voice flying ahead of him. When he and Wentworth reached the deck, the boat was already ripping through the black river at top speed for the shores of

New York City. Wentworth moved up and down the lee quarter on slow, stiff legs. He had thought that victory was in hand and now it was more remote than ever. Suppose he had destroyed one stronghold of the Chinese beast? What did that amount to beside the fact that Nita and Kirkpatrick were... He shut off his thoughts. That way lay madness and he must plan, plan, desperately.

"Your prisoner?" Flynn said as they docked at the Battery, the first words he had spoken since he had ordered the boat to Manhattan.

"A woman called White Flower," Wentworth said flatly. "Wang-ba's strongest agent."

"A pity," Flynn growled. "We could have got it out of her."

"Not without torture," Wentworth muttered dully.

Flynn barked a sharp laugh into the night. "Well?" he demanded harshly.

Wentworth stared at the soldier profile as the police limousine sped them behind shrieking sirens toward Centre Street. Flynn, he perceived, meant precisely what he implied. He would not balk even at torturing a woman to learn the truth. And Flynn was the soul of chivalry—a gentleman of the old school. Wentworth's shoulders dragged and he realized he had brought the fire arrows with him. Well, they might be useful. Any man they captured would know the potentialities of the Devil Flame for torture. Perhaps a threat....

A shiver jerked at his muscles as he stepped out into the cold wind of Centre Street. Am I catching cold? he wondered, then laughed helplessly at the prosaic thought. The truth was he was very tired. Hours and days had dragged out endlessly and all of them had been full of torture and travail and suspense… In police headquarters, he sent for Ram Singh to come, bringing clothing and guns. He dropped heavily into a chair in the familiar, big, square office of the Commissioner. He thrust his legs out toward a steam radiator hissing in the corner. Across the room, the teletype clattered and pounded. Flynn stood before it on long, braced legs, his head bowed over the paper ribbon that jerked out in little spurts….

"Got any whisky?" Wentworth asked.

"Bottom right drawer," Flynn told him, without lifting his head. "Pour me one, too."

Wentworth got up stiffly, found the bottle and two glasses. He stood with the bottle in his hand and stared at nothing. *Nita,* he thought. Good God, he should not be standing here, calmly pouring a drink. He should be searching…. But he knew this was best. Here, they would get the first news of the latest attack by Wang-ba. Heaven grant that they would recognize it immediately. Slowly, he let the amber liquor gurgle into the glasses, two stiff pegs, walked across to where Flynn stood.

"Anything?" he asked.

Flynn jerked his head in negative, took the glass. "To death!" he jeered.

WENTWORTH LOOKED into his glass. "Sure, to death!" They tossed them off. A bell jangled in the ticker and Wentworth twisted his head about, watched slow words tick out on the tape.

"Bell means homicide!" Flynn's voice started as a whisper, broke harshly.

"Brooklyn," Wentworth read. "By God, Flynn, this is it! Seven men reported dead in explosion. Army auto blown up. Five dead...."

The ticker went dead and there was a faint rattling of the windows, the echo of an explosion that was like a velvet thud. Flynn and Wentworth stared at each other, motionless through a febrile second. Then Wentworth swung toward the door. Flynn was on his heels and they went clattering down steps to the driveway entrance. Uniformed men were crowding from a door.

"I haven't got a gun," Wentworth cursed.

Flynn barked an order and handed two men's revolvers to him. They went down to the street, into the waiting limousine.

"Brooklyn," Flynn snapped. "Snyder and Bedford."

Behind them, headquarters was in turmoil. Even as the Commissioner's limousine surged forward, an emergency wagon skidded out of the police garage and went racketing down the street. Within less than a minute, they were roaring up the approach to Manhattan Bridge. The radio was speaking harshly.

"Orders are to capture at least one man alive," the voice said, coldly deliberate. "He is to be surrendered to Commissioner Flynn. Brooklyn headquarters reported blown up. All Brooklyn cars take orders direct from Manhattan. Enemy believed using explosives. Shoot any suspicious Chinese on sight. Capture at least one man alive...."

The voice droned on, order after order in smooth progression. Flynn had laid his plans well. When the attack of Wang-ba

Wentworth raised the sword to behead Commissioner Flynn!

broke, he had given a single order, and the entire police force swung into action like the piece of smoothly greased machinery that it was.

The car rocketed down the slope of Manhattan bridge. The streets were empty of traffic, except for military patrols. They were streaking eastward on courses paralleling Flynn's. Wentworth leaned from the window of the car and stared upward at the structure of the elevated railway under which they were passing, tried to keep an eye on high buildings. If Wang-ba was using his explosives as he did his Devil Flame, he probably had men posted up there with cross-bows....

Without warning, an army car ahead flew apart with a terrific blast of white flame. The police driver slewed into a side street, took another corner at top speed.

"Halt!" Commissioner Flynn barked. "The battle begins here."

CHAPTER 13
TREACHERY

TOGETHER, WENTWORTH and Flynn smashed downward, went into the dark hallway of the building. The elevator doors were locked and no one was on watch. They went up the stairs in two-step strides. Wentworth was intent only on reaching the roof, finding the men of Wang-ba.

Wentworth's lungs were panting when he reached the next to the top floor. Flynn kept pace with him, gasping for breath. They whipped open the door and started upward. Wentworth wasted breath on a curse. The air was strangely exhilarating, there was an odor of ozone… He whirled about.

"Quickly, out of here," he gasped. "Wang-ba's anesthetic gas."

He stumbled toward the door below them. Flynn was clinging to the railing, head hanging, apparently already in the grip of the gas. Wentworth tried to hold his breath, but his body clamored for air, his blood raced from the exertion of the climb. He caught hold of Flynn's arm, made one stride, toward the door, and… darkness….

Wentworth's return to his senses was as abrupt as on the previous occasion when White Flower had dropped him into the trap in the pier stronghold. He heard a voice saying: "There will be twelve heads instead of ten to deliver this evening."

The words had no meaning immediately but memory returned with a flash like flame. Twelve leads, instead of ten! Why, Good God, he was once more in the deadly power of Wang-ba! He opened his eyes and saw only dim darkness in which vague figures moved. He was in a boat.

Wentworth moved his hands cautiously, felt the wrists cut by bonds, looked about him. At his side lay he inert figure of Commissioner Flynn. He must lave absorbed a greater amount of gas. The voice he just had heard was gloating: "Twelve heads. *Aie,* it is a fitting answer to the white fools!"

"Quiet, egg of a turtle," another answered and Wentworth's muscles jerked. The White Flower! Then, it had been she who set that trap for him upon he stairs of the building on whose roof the men of Wang-ba crouched! Abruptly, he understood. It had been she who had permitted him to escape, in the estimation of Wang-ba. She sought to reinstate herself by restoring the prisoner with another to compensate for the loss of the Staten Island stronghold.

"I hope," Wentworth said clearly, "that you achieve *the mercy of Wang-ba.*"

"Ah," White Flower moved on silent feet until she stood over him. "You learn by experience, Wentworth *san*. You did not inhale much of Wang-ba's gas."

Wentworth thought bitterly that Wang-ba had been right. The very humanity of the West would prove its doom. He had saved this woman from a death she richly deserved and his reward was that she took him prisoner to die with those others whom Wang-ba had captured. Nita…? Was there any chance that Ram Singh had arrived at police headquarters in time to follow? Wentworth shook his head heavily. He had no way of telling, of course, how long he and Flynn had been in the building where they had walked into the gas trap, but it would not have been long. No, no, if there was any hope at all, it must lie with himself. Bitter laughter rose, but he held it down. He jeered at himself. Truly, Wang-ba had completely outwitted him.

IT WAS an hour later that the boat came to a halt in the chamber of the submarine that Wentworth knew so well, but this time there was no murderous attempt. They were hauled without ceremony into the forward control chamber, thrown to their knees before the turtle throne of Wang-ba. The Chinese scarcely glanced at them. He looked at White Flower.

"Very well," he said, "you have earned the mercy of Wang-ba. You may go."

Wentworth smiled bitterly at the floor on which he kneeled. He had hoped that Wang-ba would do something to arouse the hatred of White Flower.

"Throw these fools in with the rest," Wang-ba said, in his gentle voice. "In half an hour we will anchor and I will attend to them all."

Wentworth was jerked roughly to his feet and hurled presently into a chamber aft. He lost his balance, fell heavily and lay half-stunned for long minutes. Finally, he thrust himself erect.

"Nita?" he called softly.

A woman's voice uttered a glad cry, and through the darkness came the sound of stumbling feet. "Dick?" Nita whispered. "Dick, boy, did that fiend get you, too?"

Then Nita had found him in the dark. She laid her cheek against his chest. Their arms were bound behind them. He bowed his lips to her hair.

"Is there any hope at all?" Nita asked with despair in her voice.

"None," Wentworth answered. "In a half hour, we will anchor and Wang-ba will 'attend' to us."

"A half hour?" It was Kirkpatrick's voice speaking in the darkness. "Not much time, Dick. Any chance at all?"

Wentworth doubted it.

Kirkpatrick laughed, naturally enough. "Sounds a little crazy," he said, "but you're right enough. He probably won't permit us to die... nicely." He tried to speak in a normal tone of voice, but there was the harshness of strain in his words.

Nita's head was on Wentworth's shoulder. He could feel the tension of her body. They were like that when the lights went on with blinding suddenness. The door was opened and four men with revolvers stood behind White Flower.

"Wentworth, *san*, you are summoned to the Presence."

Wentworth felt Nita's body tense and he saw an odd excitement in the eyes of White Flower. The lips were smiling in the cruel way he remembered.

"Good-bye," he said lightly and crossed the chamber toward the door. White Flower greeted him with an enigmatic smile, with a gun muzzle pressed against his backbone.

"You claim your will is stronger than that of Wang-ba," she whispered. "There will be an opportunity to see!"

WENTWORTH'S HEART sprang high with hopefulness at what White Flower prophesied, but immediately afterward he frowned in doubt. He did not doubt his own strength, but what effect would that previous experience have on him? It was said that once a man's will bowed to another's, he could never resist.

Wentworth went into the forward chamber of the submarine with his head high, his bearing confident. Wang-ba nodded to him politely, shaking his own hands gently before his heart.

"Greetings, Wentworth, *san*," he said, "It has come to my ears that you claim your will to be the stronger. Is this so?"

Wentworth made a small, deprecating gesture. "I do not care to boast."

"Ah, yes," Wang-ba murmured, "another of those charming little Western world weaknesses."

Wentworth felt his heart bounding high and strong within him. He was aware of the eyes of White Flower, of the battering regard from Wang-ba's black orbs. He smiled slightly, but inwardly he was tense with excitement. Would Wang-ba submit to a duel of wills? If he did....

Wang-ba's voice ripped out suddenly in Chinese. Wentworth's mind, intent on other things, did not for a moment grasp his meaning, but he heard White Flower gasp, heard her deep voice rap out in harsh curses. A hand met flesh viciously and she was silent. Wentworth looked at her and saw that her arms had been twisted painfully behind her and bound. She was glaring at the man on the turtle throne. "I suspected your mercy," she told him calmly, "and I have prepared for it."

Wang-ba leaned forward slightly, his black eyes widening as he looked at her. "What do you mean, my pretty little almond blossom?"

White Flower laughed at him derisively. She looked over his head and held her eyes there, unmoving. Wang-ba leaned back on his throne.

"You still are entitled to my mercy," he said gently. "You will merely be beheaded with the rest. You will notice that the ceiling of this salon is quite high, high enough for you to wield the sword, eh, Wentworth *san?*"

Wentworth was rigid with sudden anger and apprehension. What the devil did Wang-ba mean? Wang-ba's eyes were still sleepy upon his.

"Yes, yes, Wentworth *san,*" he said. "You have challenged my will so I say to you that you shall behead not only White Flower, but all these others, including the light of your own eyes who left your arms but a moment ago."

Wentworth's arms were still held by two of the Chinese who had escorted him into the throne room. They were powerful and no trickery of his would suffice to free him. If he did escape for a moment, there were two other men there beside White Flower, and there were no weapons... He forced himself to relax, drew in his breath deeply and strongly.

"I say to you, Wang-ba," he announced flatly, "that I shall not!" AS SIMPLY as that was the battle of their wills joined. Immediately, there was utter silence in the room. Wentworth was aware that White Flower was watching him, watching with unwinking eyes. Truly, she had gambled greatly on his strength! Wang-ba sat motionless upon his turtle throne and looked into Wentworth's eyes.

Through long moments, nothing happened. Wentworth could feel tension mounting in his body. He set his thoughts on one thing: "I will not submit." His fists knotted at his sides. The muscles in his neck hardened and grew rigid. Perspiration popped out beneath his eyes, across his upper lip. But he did not move his eyes from Wang-ba.

Nor was Wang-ba entirely calm. Wentworth could see the rigidity of the man's body as he concentrated on the effort of overcoming his prisoner with his will. His breath came more quickly, and his hands clutched on the arms of his turtle throne.

"My will above thine!" he thundered.

Abruptly, Wentworth's eyes closed, the tension went out of his body. He swayed on his feet and when his eyes opened, they were dull, without vision.

"My will above thine!" Wang-ba whispered. "You are no

longer Wentworth *san*. You are the executioner of Wang-ba. Who are you?"

"The executioner of Wang-ba." Like his eyes, Wentworth's voice was dull.

"I have given you a task this night!" Wang-ba's voice rose triumphantly and White Flower, on her knees, swayed and moaned. "The task I have given my executioner is the lopping off of twelve heads. What is your task, executioner?"

Wentworth's lips moved stiffly. "I am to behead twelve persons."

"Bring the prisoners to the executioner," Wang-ba ordered. Feet shuffled away down the corridor to the rear. Presently, they returned and the eleven prisoners were lined up beside White Flower.

"Governor Kirkpatrick," Wang-ba's voice was honeyed now. "I want you to look upon my newest executioner. I have but recently recruited him and it may be that his work is a little imperfect. Therefore, I shall give him a bit of practice upon some of the lesser dignitaries before he operates upon you. I have always thought that police were the lowest of the low. Right, Commissioner Flynn?"

Flynn's soldier's face glowered at Wang-ba, then turned to Wentworth. Resolutely, he stepped forward. "Wentworth," he said sharply. "What's wrong?"

Wentworth looked through him with stony eyes. He said, slowly, "I am the executioner of Wang-ba."

Wang-ba chuckled with his face impassive. "He has learned his lesson well. Down on your knees, vermin!"

Two Chinese seized Flynn's arms, forced him down on his knees, forced him to bend his neck forward for the headsman's blade.

"Give my executioner his sword!"

A Chinese came forward with a short, heavy sword whose blade was wide and razor-sharp. He put it into Wentworth's hand. Without hesitation, the Spider swung it high over his head, stood above the bowed neck of Flynn.

"Dick!" Nita cried. "In God's name!"

THE SWORD started down, but mid-way in its course, it swerved. The Chinese who was holding Flynn's left arm took the edge of the blade in his skull and spilled, lifeless to the floor. The headsman's sword was wrenched free and the second Chinese died.

"Wentworth!" Wang-ba trumpeted. "Stop it, fool. You are my executioner and...."

"Up and at them, Flynn!" Wentworth roared. "Those two dead men have weapons!"

Nita raised her voice in a joyful cry and Kirkpatrick lunged forward, dived head-first against the belly of a Chinese who had drawn back a knife to throw. Wentworth's face was no longer lifeless, but twisted with rage. He was everywhere at once, never still, and the heavy headsman's sword flashed before him with the speed of a rapier. Five Chinese were already dead and the others fled in terror before the assault of a man who was, supposedly, the plaything of their master....

Wentworth whirled, panting, toward the throne, his headsman's sword raised high to finish Wang-ba. For once, the

Chinese sense of humor had been betrayed. Wang-ba had trusted his willpower too far, had planned to have Wentworth execute all his friends, his sweetheart, then let him recover his right senses for a brief while before he, too, was killed. But Wentworth had tricked him, had pretended to succumb to his will....

"The Devil Flame!" White Flower cried. "The Devil Flame!"

Wentworth saw that the throne was empty, whirled toward the sound of the woman's voice. She was plunging, almost headfirst, across the room, toward where Wang-ba crouched half-hidden behind a steel column to whose side was fastened a wheel. His hands were already upon the wheel, twisting it.... White Flower plunged not toward the wheel, but toward a jet fastened to the column and even as she lunged forward, a tiny tongue of green Devil Flame licked from the opening.

Wentworth whirled the headsman's sword over his head, once, twice, in a glittering circle. The flame was belching forth in a torch of intolerable heat, but it was not reaching as far as where Wentworth stood. It was wrapping White Flower's body in a tower of green fire! She was screaming in incredible agony, but she did not move from the flame.

With a final, whistling circle, Wentworth released the headsman's sword. It flew, straight as an arrow, with all the impetus of Wentworth's long arms behind it. Wang-ba, too late, realized that his flames would not suffice and tried to leap aside. The sword point caught him in the chest and sheared through flesh and bone, plunged home to its very hilt! Under the surge of power, Wang-ba was hurled back against the wall and for a dozen heart-beats, he stood there, swaying, his head wrenched back in agony. Then he pitched forward upon the floor, dead....

Even before he fell, Wentworth was darting forward, circling that tongue of gruesome flame. White Flower had fallen, silent at last, to the floor. Wentworth reached the wheel, spun it and the Devil Flame ceased. But he could not extinguish the fire that throbbed like a living torment against the steel walls and over the charred body of White Flower.

Wentworth stood, swaying from the intolerable heat. Commissioner Flynn had already found the way to the conning tower and was marshaling the prisoners upward to the pure cold air of the night and safety. Wentworth reeled away from the wall, turned to stare down upon the body of Wang-ba. He felt a hand upon his arm, turned to find Nita tugging frantically. "Hurry, Dick!" she shouted.

WENTWORTH REELED across the chamber toward the base of the conning tower where Flynn seized his arm and dragged him upward. The air was a caress to his burning lungs. They were within fifty feet of the shore and already boats were putting out. In the foremost, Wentworth saw the turbaned head of Ram Singh. A spear of green flame licked its point up through the conning tower....

"I still don't understand," Wentworth said softly, "why Wang-ba trusted to his will power to subdue me. He had found out once before that he could not... unless there were drugs."

"There were supposed to be drugs," Nita told him, pressing close into the circle of his arms. "That girl... who died... gave me something for you. She said that you were her vengeance against Wang-ba."

Nita held out her hand and in the darkness, something caught the light of the green flame and glittered wickedly. It was a tiny feathered dart such as the first time had subjugated Wentworth to Wang-ba's will.

"She was supposed to prick you with it, Dick," Nita whispered. She shuddered. "She was so brave!"

Wentworth fingered the dart. He smiled, thinking: The East has its weaknesses, too!

www.ingramcontent.com/pod-product-compliance
Lightning Source LLC
Chambersburg PA
CBHW020439180626
46812CB00003B/1308